Letters to Jonny
Journeying to Bethlehem by different roads

Letters to Jonny
Journeying to Bethlehem by different roads

Chris Chivers
with responses by Anjum Anwar

2016

Letters to Jonny: Journeying to Bethlehem by different roads — jointly published by the Rev. Dr. Ashish Amos of the Indian Society for Promoting Christian Knowledge (ISPCK), Post Box 1585, Kashmere Gate, Delhi-110006 and USPG, Harling House, 47-51 Great Suffolk Street, London, SE1 0BS

Online Order: http://ispck.org.in/book.php

Also available on amazon.in

ISBN: 978-81-8465-559-9

Cover photo credit: Leah Gordon

Laser typeset by

ISPCK, Post Box 1585, 1654, Madarsa Road, Kashmere Gate, Delhi-110006 • *Tel:* 23866323

e-mail: ashish@ispck.org.in • ella@ispck.org.in
website: www.ispck.org.in

For our sons,

Jonathan Joseph Chivers and Danyal Ahmed

and for our parents,

Ernest and Margaret Chivers,
Anwar and Rafiqui Hussain

Contents

Contents

Acknowledgements

Thanks to the Revd Dr Stephen Srikantha for all his help with the editing for publication of these letters and the responses that accompany them for Advent 2016, since they were originally conceived and first used as an on-line audio and written resource for USPG in Advent 2015; to Leah Gordon for the cover photograph and for recording the original audio resource; to the Staff of USPG, especially Rachel Parry and Janette O'Neill, for their inspiration and encouragement; to the Very Revd Christopher Armstrong, Dean of Blackburn until this year, who first encouraged our work to develop and enabled it to flourish; to the churchwardens and parishioners of John Keble Church, Mill Hill; the staff and students of Westcott House, Cambridge; and to the ISPCK production team.

Across faiths and world views, the letters chart a journey that faces tough realities yet finds humans also at their most resilient even when they are often at their most vulnerable.

Responding to this, a Muslim perspective seeks to enhance the fabric of a journey that embraces such a rich diversity of human experience.

Anjum Anwar and Chris Chivers
June 2016

Preface

*W*hat may we say with confidence to our children about the state of the world this Advent?

What true message of hope can see us through to Christmas, in a way that does justice to the reality of human experience?

What can inspire us to live fully and love meaningfully in the face of terrorism and war?

These are some of the questions we seek to explore as friends through these daily meditations for Advent written by a Christian with responses from a Muslim.

The meditations take the form of letters addressed by a father to his youngest son, nine year old Jonathan, and they emerge from visits to Tanzania, South Africa, the United Arab Emirates, India, Pakistan, Kenya and Sri Lanka.

Weaving narratives from the visits around an exploration of the first few chapters of Matthew and Luke's Gospels, the letters set out to 'discover how to be human now', in the words of WH Auden written in the midst of the Second World War.

Saturday 26 November: Introduction

*D*ear Jonny,

I don't know if you'll remember, but a while ago in church we were coming back from Communion, and as a baby let out a huge scream you turned to me and said something extraordinary. 'That', you exclaimed, 'was the sound God made when he came into the world!'

I wasn't sure whether it was a thought that popped into your head or whether it was something you'd heard... perhaps in a sermon?

It's actually something I once heard Michael Mayne, a great spiritual writer, priest and friend, say when people were getting irritated with a baby crying out to be fed during a Communion service.

Perhaps it was just a case of great minds thinking alike!

But it's a good place to begin the first of some letters that I'm going to write to you as a father's Advent and Christmas gift to a son who asks lots of questions about the world and what our place as human beings is within it. I hope at least some of these will point some way forward for you, even if they don't answer all your questions.

So I'm going to write every day between now and Christmas Day.

What, you may wonder, prompts me to do so?

I think there are three reasons.

I've already hinted at the first: there are things you ask as a human being that deserve at least some thoughts towards an answer, not least because you watch the news, see many of the tensions of the world and wonder, like the rest of us, why and where it's all going. So, I'll try to share some stories with you from my recent travels and I hope this might help.

Those travels are the second reason for writing. They've taken me away from you, often for longish periods. And, I know you haven't found this easy. The least I can do is to try properly to explain what I've been up to and what I've learned about being human along the way.

'To discover how to be human now is the reason I follow the star', says one of the Magi in WH Auden's poem *For the Time Being*. Auden wrote this during the dark days of the Second World War. The poem tries to reflect on what the story of God coming into the world means for a world screaming out its pain and problems.

I'm going to try and tell you some of the story of how God came into the world as it's written in the opening chapters of two books in the Bible that we call the Gospels. The word means good news and we're going to focus on the Gospels by Luke and Matthew. As I tell you about how God came into the world, I'm going to weave in the stories of other people who've come into the world, just like you and me.

I'm doing this, thirdly, because when I visited Delhi a couple of years ago, you'll remember that I met with Anglicans from around the world. We'd all been brought together by USPG, the Anglican Mission Agency. They all said they wanted us to explore some of the difficulties of being human, especially as experienced by people who express their belief in God. So you'll find in these letters quite a lot about different faiths and 'world views' (that means different ways of looking at things).

I hope to make each letter no longer than this one. But I know that I'm going to fail in this. There's just too much to say. So bear with me: you know me well enough by now!

I'm going to add some words at the end of every letter before I sign off. These will be words to pray and think about as we journey to Bethlehem and beyond.

Here, then, is a prayer which I hope might help as we set out:

God of a thousand names
we bring to you a thousand questions
about the world
about being human
about love and hate
peace and violence
wealth and poverty.
You are the answer to them.
This we know
because the sound you made
when you came into the world
was the sound each of us makes.
Help us to learn the truth of your life

in the stories you give us

of yourself

and of our neighbours.

With love, Daddy

Dear Chris,

Thank you for finding such an innovative way of telling us all, insiders and outsiders, the story of Advent.

Nothing is more important than learning how to be human, and who can teach us this better than a child. I am thinking about Jonny at this point, who asks questions of you, and no doubt causes you embarrassment too! Difficult questions have to be asked.

I am looking forward to learning about the birth of Jesus through your letters. However, more importantly, I am looking forward to reading these letters written by a father to his son — letters from a father who happens to be one of the finest Christians that I know and respect as a friend and brother in faith.

My blessings for all that you do for humanity at large!

'My humanity is bound up in yours, for we can only be human together.' —
Archbishop Emeritus Desmond Tutu

Yours, Anjum

Sunday 27 November

Dear Jonny,

It's Advent Sunday and the start of a new Christian year. This means we begin to follow the story of Jesus again.

We do it in a yearly cycle because if you keep coming back to a story – especially the story of God made human - you see new things each time you return.

Traditionally, people used to begin Advent Sunday by reading what's called the genealogy at the start of Matthew's account of Jesus. A genealogy is really a family tree. Some churches have windows with what are called Jesse trees in them. I remember the Jesse window of the Eastern Lady Chapel in Bristol Cathedral from my time as a chorister there. It depicts the family tree of Jesus. Beginning with Abraham it tries to show how everyone is related to everyone else in the Bible and how therefore everyone is ultimately related to Jesus.

In South Africa they have a saying in isiXhosa, *Umuntu ngumuntu ngabantu.* Roughly translated, this means 'I am because you are: you are because we are.' In other words, 'a person is a person through other persons.' The English poet and priest,

John Donne, once said 'no man is an island.' By this he seems to be saying that no one can exist without other people. You'll remember that at the Eucharist we say 'Though we are many we are one body'. Muslims talk about the *Ummah*, the powerful reality that unites all of them.

Travelling to Kenya, India, South Africa, Sri Lanka, Tanzania and the United Arab Emirates with Anjum Anwar has reminded me once again of two things. We are one. We are all human. We cry and laugh. We have children. We seek to feed and clothe them, to educate them, to enable them to fulfil their dreams and to be fully alive. However, though this is what we share in common, we're also very different.

If you read the genealogy in Matthew chapter 1 (verses 1-17) carefully you may discover this for yourself. As you read, the characters you encounter are pretty surprising.

Abraham is an amazing man of faith. But he nearly cut the throat of his son Isaac, the father of Jacob, who got his position in the line by cheating his blind father. Jacob was in turn cheated. In the old language, as you hear the list read, the word begat is used. So and so begat so and so. This is really a way of saying 'is the father of'. But as each person begets another we also learn that the list of swindlers, violent and not-so-worthy people grows!

When I was a student, I heard one of the best sermons of my life on this genealogy. It was by a remarkable monk called Herbert McCabe. He ended the sermon by pointing out that 'Jesus did not belong to the nice world of nice people' we often think of as the world of those who go to church. He belonged to a family of murderers, cheats, cowards, adulterers and liars. He belonged to a world of sinners, the world of you and me.

People get things badly wrong. You are shielded for now from the worst of this. But when you are older you will sadly realise not just how awful everyone else can be but just how awful you too can sometimes be. You may not end up cheating people but you may think about doing so. This is also called being human, in need of help, fallen. It's that help that Advent is all about. So here's another prayer that I hope might help you think about what I've written today:

Lord Jesus,
I know that I can get things wrong
make bad decisions
be unkind
unhelpful
untruthful.
But I also know that I can do good
help people
make them smile
show them love.
Teach me to draw strength
from belonging to my faith
and from being like all my neighbours, simply human.
Show me how to build bridges of friendship
that make the world a better place.

With love, Daddy

Dear Chris,

Advent! Waiting, expecting and preparing for the 'coming'. We Muslims do not celebrate the birth of Jesus (pbuh) in the same way as Christian friends, but we, too, are waiting, expecting and preparing for the return of the Messiah Jesus. We believe he will return to earth one day and make it a place where justice will prevail for all. Both our communities believe in the return of Jesus, but of course we have differences of opinion on his status – for me a prophet of God, and to you God, Son and the Holy Ghost!

I love the isiXhosa saying which you quote Chris in your letter to Jonny, 'I am because you are; you are because we are.' We are connected to each other through the genealogy of Abraham, Moses, Jesus and, for me, Muhammad (pbuh). This is a family tree which binds humanity! Sadly, when we look around, it seems like we have lost our humanity. But losing humanity is nothing new. Take Tamar, for example, who is mentioned in the genealogy of Jesus. She was burnt alive thousands of years ago. Sadly, we witness similar atrocities in our own times.

How easy it is to work with those who commit no sin, how difficult it is to work with those who cheat, commit adultery, terrorism, lie and cheat! As you quote Herbert McCabe, Chris, 'Jesus did not belong to the nice world of nice people', but he belonged to the world of you and me! Our work is not with those who agree with each other, or are nice to each other, but with those who have differences of opinions and are hurt by each other. We are humans and we get things wrong but we also have a blue print to get things right, the blue print is the living word of Abraham, Moses, Jesus and Muhammad (pbut). Ameen!

'Every prophet and saint has a path but it all leads to One God. All paths are the same.' – Rumi

Yours, Anjum

Monday 28 November

Dear Jonny,

Yesterday, we looked a little bit at the start of Matthew's Gospel – his telling of the good news of Jesus coming into the world. The good news for all those cheats and swindlers, murderers and cowards is that God loves them enough to come as a baby.

Today, we turn to Luke's Gospel. In fact, we're going to spend quite a lot of time now with the first two chapters of it. They paint a diptych (that's a picture with two halves). We'll see how as we go along.

But for now, we meet a man who also knows his place in the order of things. He's an old man called Zechariah, of the priestly order of Abijah. His wife Elizabeth is descended from Aaron, the older brother of Moses. They are already among what you might call the in-crowd. They're respected by the people who go to the temple. They live in Jerusalem. But they have a big problem. They're old and they don't have a son. There's been no begetting yet and if they don't beget soon their line will end!

But an angel appears when Zechariah is busy doing his priestly thing.

Not surprisingly, he's completely terrified and then shocked by what the angel says: his aged wife is going to have a baby.

The original listeners of this story would have thought, 'Ah, it's just like Abraham and Sarah having a baby when she was so old, so is the story starting all over again?' They would have been right to think this because a new story was indeed beginning, the story that would see another baby born to save the world.

But for now, Zechariah is busy trying to take in what he's hearing about his own wife and son-to-be. He's told that his son will have the power of Elijah. As he was one of the great heroes of the Bible, that too was quite a thing to say. Zechariah is told that his son will be filled with the Holy Spirit – and as the Spirit breathed on the waters to start the story of the whole universe, that's another big claim! He won't drink – which is what Aaron's sons promised they wouldn't do when they came to worship, and that's Elizabeth's side of the family of course. So the story sets all sorts of bells ringing for its listeners. It's even like the moment when Samson's birth is announced in the book of Judges.

Poor Zechariah, he knows all these stories. He knows they ought to be helping him to believe what's being said.

But he doesn't believe it. He's dumbstruck as they say. Indeed, perhaps that word came from this story because the angel says that Zechariah will be struck dumb because of his lack of belief. So he's not able to tell his friends anything when he comes out of the place of worship. All he can do is flap his arms around and go home.

What does it all mean?

A lot of it is symbolism. It's a series of triggers all designed to show that if God did something like this before, then, we ought to be paying special attention to what he's doing now. But as we'll see when we go on to think about the next time an angel makes an announcement – which is the one you'll know better because it's made to Mary – Luke is making another point.

We've had an announcement to elderly folk who are insiders. Next, we will get one to a girl just a few years older than you. A girl who doesn't live in Jerusalem but is far from the centre of things, in a marginal country village where nothing very much of significance happens. So, Luke's point is to show the old way of looking at things needs a jolly good shake up. Who better to do this than someone like John the Baptist, shouting his way about the wilderness to the place where he pours water over people and invites them to turn their lives round and change?

It's dramatic stuff. But it's a story that's completely relevant to what's happening in the world now because it feels like we've all been living through a time of tectonic shift. I know I can use the word tectonic because earthquakes, volcanoes and tectonic plates are all things you've learned about – do you remember the time you made your own volcano with baking soda? Who could forget that?!

You were born in 2007, in the shadow of a decade – a period of ten years – which saw some truly appalling events. It's tempting to list them. Yet, as people right round the world will be reading what I'm writing to you, I don't want simply to choose the ones that I remember from the time your mother and brothers were living with me in South Africa and Britain. So I'm going to leave it open for you to discover what happened and for other readers to think about things from what's called their perspective.

That's the last point I want to make before I sign off today. You see, we all live in particular places and where we live, with whom we live, how we live, play and pray, what we eat, read, and see, these all affect how we see the world: what we think is important and what we choose to ignore. That's something I hope you'll bear in mind as I try to explain to you in the letters that follow how other people see things. I can't claim to do that fully, of course, because I'm not them. We can only really tell our own story. But, hopefully, I've learned to listen well enough – better than Zechariah at least! – to be able to give you an impression which honours their words and feelings. So pray with me as we go forward:

> Loving God,
> our Hindu friends remind us
> that we have two ears and only one mouth.
> Help us to look and to listen
> with care and compassion.
> In this Advent season
> help us to wait before we speak.

With love, Daddy

Dear Chris,

Zechariah / Zakariayah is a prophet of God whose story we both recognise, and whose son, John the Baptist (prophet Yahya in Islam), we both honour. Both our faith communities see the same person through our own Scriptures. Was Zechariah 'struck dumb' or, as it says in my own Scriptures, was he simply keeping silent in order to reflect more about all that had happened?

God said: 'O Zakariyah! Verily, We give you the glad tidings of a son. His name will be John. We have given that name to none before him.'

He said: 'My Lord! How can I have a son, when my wife is barren, and I have reached extreme old age.'

God said: 'So (it will be). Your Lord says, It is easy for Me. Certainly I have created you before, when you had been nothing.'

Zakariyah said: 'My Lord! Appoint for me a sign.'

He said: 'Your sign is that you shall not speak unto mankind for three nights, though having no bodily defect.'

And, of course, we see a similar story unfolding when an announcement is made to Mary (mother of Christ) too! We can see similarities in our stories but, as you say Chris, we can only really tell our own story. We must, however, learn to keep silent and listen to the other too, only then will we understand.

'Keeping silent is the language of God, all else is poor translation.' – Rumi

Yours, Anjum

Tuesday 29 November

Dear Jonny,

You'll remember that we were thinking about Zechariah – and his elderly, now pregnant, wife Elizabeth. You'll remember too that in the story they represent religious people, insiders as it were, and that God thinks these religious folk all need a shake up?

Well, if you followed all that, then perhaps what I write next will make some sense.

The last few years, as I hinted, have been very difficult for people right across the globe. Wars and rumours of wars – that's how one of the other Gospel writers, Mark, describes them – violence and terrorism, natural disaster and plague, famine and disease, they've all been part of what people have experienced.

Anjum and I stayed just above the beach in Galle on the coast of Sri Lanka. We imagined the waves of the Tsunami that struck there the day after Christmas in 2004 as we walked along the beach. Speaking to people who lost loved ones and their homes and shops on that day brought us close to tears. When we visited Lahore, we wept as we listened to the story of what happened one Sunday morning when people going to church in a place in northern Pakistan called Peshawar were killed by suicide bombers. These bombers claimed to be Muslims. But Islam means 'peace'!

We had wanted to go to Peshawar. Anjum, as someone born in Pakistan, would probably have been safe there. But my pink skin was thought to make me unsafe. So, a group of people had travelled hundreds of miles just to tell us their story. Just the thought of that long journey makes me cry now. Later on in these letters we will meet the Magi who travelled hundreds of miles because they'd heard the story of a newborn king. I was frankly embarrassed by the fact that this group of men and women from Peshawar had travelled to meet us because we couldn't travel to meet them.

They brought with them a Peshawar Cross – the edge of each arm is fashioned with a set of thorns. I often hold it and pray with it as I think of what they told us.

One of the issues behind what happened there is what we call urbanisation. It sometimes goes with other words which sound similar: homogenisation, globalisation and secularisation. You'll remember a few years ago that David Fanshawe came to stay with us just a little while before he died. He's the composer who went round Africa and Polynesia collecting what's called indigenous music. He was recording the music that different groups of people have developed for themselves over hundreds, even thousands of years. You may remember him saying, however, that much of the music he collected in Africa now only exists in his recordings. The communities who sang what he recorded have moved from villages to cities.

One of the big stories in Africa over the twentieth century was the way in which a whole continent became more urbanised. Now, of course, big cities have lots of advantages. They mean that large numbers of people ought to have better access to food, work, education and healthcare. In part this is true. But it can also mean a whole lot of other realities. Village communities with their own distinctive traditions can have these destroyed when their citizens move to the city and city life takes over.

In earlier letters I mentioned that we are one. There's an upside to this. We belong together. We rely on each other. We are meant to care for each other. Yet, there's a downside to this when being one means being forced to be one and the same. We are all human – but each of us is unique. Sometimes what's called homogenisation – fitting people into the same mould – destroys the uniqueness even as it tries to emphasise the things we rightly hold in common.

Where all this is forced and accompanied by what we call globalisation, a few brands, products and companies dominate the world and make us all eat the same food, buy the same clothes, use the same gadgets and, in your case, play the same online games. Where it's also accompanied by secularisation – which means at one level that differences of faith or belief, of culture or history should be suppressed because we are all the same – a huge amount of tension results.

Imagine, for one moment, if I made you stop speaking English and made you speak only Shona – not a word of which you yet know? Imagine, in addition to this, if I said that you could only eat noodles, you could only play American Football and watch Tanzanian television? It's a silly picture isn't it? But something of that silliness lies at the heart of the world right now, a world seemingly not able to live with difference, a world where difference becomes a problem and a cause of violence, even. Yet, this is also a world where many are forced – ironically – to embrace a confusing array of differences that aren't their own.

If I'm making sense to you, then you'll perhaps see how this relates back to poor old Zechariah. The angel was forcing him out of his comfort zone. Things were going to change. His wife was going to have a baby. He was going to be a dad. The baby would grow up and scare the living daylights out of the neighbours. Some of this was good and necessary!

But forced change isn't always so easy to deal with.

When Anjum and I spent time with Muslims in Kenya we often heard from people who felt that their traditional culture had been invaded, replaced or even destroyed. 'The Macdonaldisation of the world,' is how one person put it. 'Why must we all be the same? We feel like women wearing short western dresses put pressure on our veiled daughters. Will they end up behaving the same way as a result?', said another. You see, for change to be lasting it has to be organic. It has to have its own pace. When it's forced, what tends to happen is that people retreat into what they know – which is often not as much as they suppose they know – and stick to this 'thin' knowledge. Then, ignorant of their own tradition, as well as of anyone else's, they can't handle the differences they see elsewhere. This is because they haven't actually got the faintest idea what they are meant to think and believe themselves.

It's complex, isn't it? This probably means it's time for prayer!

Lord,
it's confusing to live in a world
where there's such pressure to be the same
while we're also often told we must be different
from the way we are!
Help us to root ourselves in you
and to know that the story of your love
will sustain, challenge and transform us.
With love, Daddy

Dear Chris,

How do we teach our children about religion, when religion becomes a commodity to be sold in the market place? Isn't this what has happened to Christianity and isn't this what Muslims should be afraid of — perhaps Muslims are already on a similar journey? The Advent story begins four Sundays before Christmas, but sadly, our shopping centres have far too many Christmas trees up, with sale items trying to attract people to commit to spending money they do not have.

During our travels we came across those who have little but they seem so content with their lives. Don't get me wrong, they have aspirations to acquire more - particularly given that the world makes possessions so enticing! But being amongst the people affected by the destruction on the beach in Galle, or the reality of Kibera, one of the largest slums in Nairobi, made me realise what I was missing in my world.

In these places human relationships are far more important than anything the market malls could offer. Being there made me want that contentment! I will never forget the angelic face of a child in Kibera whose penetrating eyes seemed to be demanding to know why she walked bare-feet, without the educational and health facilities that I take for granted. What is her future in this slum? Who is responsible for her plight? And all I could do was to shed a tear and wonder where we have gone so wrong. Is this the cost of 'progress'?

We had to endure much pain in Lahore as we listened to the stories of Christians who are being hurt because of their faith. Their stories put me, a Muslim, out of my comfort zone. I had to confront my own faith community members and question their actions towards a minority faith, for I am led to believe that 'the character of a nation is recognised from how it treats its minorities.' How can anyone be persecuted for their beliefs? May be we all need to go back to our traditions and Scriptures to learn what God really wants us to do. I guess this is what Advent is all about:

waiting and reflecting, not necessarily just about ourselves, but also about those who are in difficulties.

> *'Words are a pretext. It is the inner bond that draws one person to another, not words.' – Rumi*

Yours, Anjum

Wednesday 30 November

Dear Jonny,

I wondered if I'd made it more complicated than it is in what I wrote yesterday…

But adults are at their worst when they pretend that everything can be made more simple – it can't be.

I've been to Zanzibar, an island off the coast of Tanzania. It's actually part of Tanzania, but there's been an ongoing dispute about how much a part of Tanzania Zanzibar in reality is. Historically – not least because of the Arabic trading routes along that part of coastal Africa – Islam has been very strong. Traders came by boat. They were Muslims. They built mosques, grew communities around them, influenced the language of the region. There is much Arabic in kishSwahili which is the predominant language. On mainland Tanzania the experience of trading is different. You'll notice that people trading or moving around in order to work, this phenomenon keeps cropping up in these letters. Also, the way that mainland Tanzania was colonised gives Christianity a majority faith voice that it lacks in Zanzibar. That said – and this point is really important – members of different faith communities have lived peacefully with one another for hundreds of years in Zanzibar. Indeed, the present Bishop of Zanzibar's own family shows that the relationship is much closer. He is a Christian, of course, but from a Muslim family. Some of his close relatives are Muslims. This is not uncommon. In Cape Town, one of the churchwardens at the cathedral where we worshipped when I was a priest there came from a similar family. So, contrary to some of the debate about migrants that you've picked up on in the UK, there are communities around the world which have hundreds of years' worth of experience that is really positive when it comes to faiths and cultures rubbing up against one another.

I'm sorry that I'm having to stop often to define words as we go along. But those two words, faith and culture, need some explication because they're often unhelpfully confused. One way to think about them was brought home visibly to me by a priest in Zanzibar who wore what many people might have seen as Muslim clothing. That would, however, be completely the wrong way to describe it. He wore that type of clothing – including the headdress which helped him to identify with Zanzibar culture – while remaining, of course, without any shadow of doubt, a Christian.

Every faith – every set of beliefs – is expressed through culture, language, clothing, ritual, colour, music, art and architecture. These may be very distinctive in different places. We used to tease the last Archbishop of Cape Town about his mitre surrounded by animal skin. 'Beauty, not cruelty', the dean used to say. But beyond the teasing, the fact that he wore it made a serious point which is that Christianity in Africa is African, not simply some European import. In Sri Lanka, when in procession, the Anglican bishops are escorted by the sort of ceremonial fans that one might expect to see in Buddhist processions. This is not surprising because Sri Lanka's predominant cultural context is Buddhist. In the hills between a tea plantation and the most luscious fruit trees you can imagine, Anjum and I visited a church whose candles were like those in a Buddhist temple, whose doorway was heralded by the sort of ceremonial slab on which a sacred greeting is inscribed. You'd find such a doorway in a Buddhist context. In the Cathedral of Christ the Living Saviour, Colombo, the whole building – its octagonal shape, its vistas and lattice walls – is designed to honour Sri Lanka's dominant culture. The point I'm making here, may be seen in Blackburn where you were born. It's a town with well over forty mosques. Each of them relates, pretty much, to a village in the Indian subcontinent from which the originators of the mosque came. They wanted a place to practice their faith. But they also wanted the mosque to be a community centre in which their culture was celebrated and the experience of life they'd left behind was kept alive.

Now, here is the nub, as they say. Often what happens is that people are very good at keeping their cultures alive and less good at keeping their faiths as alive. When this happens there's a sort of crisis of identity. As Zechariah and Elizabeth knew well, faiths give identity. They teach us what it means to be human. Yet, when this aspect is played down and culture becomes more of the focus, then, the tension I spoke about in the last letter comes to the fore. People aren't sure what they are meant to believe so they make sure that at least they all look the same. That's too simplistic a way of putting it but it's close to the truth.

We weren't in Zanzibar long enough to judge the situation there but we did see an Anglican culture which emphasised strongly colonial rituals of how to celebrate the Eucharist, for example. At the same time, it looked as though a new sort of colonialism was being imported when it came to preaching: you could see the influence of the 'prosperity Gospel' of North America (which, basically, encourages us to believe that God will reward us with material comfort) and very little of what one might think of as classic Anglican identity. Similarly, we saw Muslims, who'd followed all the Qu'ranic injunctions about honouring Christians and lived for hundreds of years peacefully with their Christian neighbours, now finding themselves caught up in the influence of a misreading of Islam that made Christians the enemy.

Indeed, Anjum and I were there to help the Anglican clergy correct a strong impression they'd received from an outside agency that their Muslim neighbours were out to get them!

Oh dear, I fear I've let you down on the story front – just a few snatches. Let's see if I can do better tomorrow. In the meantime, there's a lot to pray about from today:

Lord Jesus,
    born into the Palestinian culture of your times
    which was also shaped by an occupying power
    as by the power of traders and travellers:
    help us to notice differences of culture and faith.
    Teach us to learn to celebrate not denigrate them,
    give us wisdom to know good from bad faith
    and the courage only and ever to encourage the good.
With love, Daddy

Dear Chris,

I guess religion requires some kind of a vehicle to express itself, and culture is that vehicle. As long as the basics of any faith are intact, people living in different parts of the world will adapt to their environment. I remember once going to India during the Christmas period and, because I had two women in my team and they were both Christians, I thought we should go to the local church! We turned up early in the morning on Christmas

Day and were confronted with a massive statute of Jesus (pbuh). However, he was not on the cross. Rather, he was sitting in the lotus position, very much like Buddha! Now that was different, I thought, but to my surprise, once we entered the church, there were no chairs. In fact men sat on one side and women sat on the other. All the women had head coverings and everyone sat on the floor.

It was the same in Zanzibar. Christian and Muslim women dressed in similar attire and people ate the same kind of food because culturally they have so much in common. I guess Africa had its own religion and culture before colonization and people lived together – indeed it still does. However, in Zanzibar and Cape Town we found that it was always the outsiders who caused most damage to community relations. The Western world has presented Africa as a continent that needs to be 'rescued', a non-civilisation that needs the white man's 'god'.

In Cape Town, Christians, Muslims, Jews and people of other faiths came together to address a common problem: apartheid. We found a similar story in Sri Lanka too, where women have taken the initiative to address some of the issues created by 30 years of war with the Tamil Tigers.

Conflicts in Zanzibar, South Africa and Sri Lanka gave their communities an opportunity to reflect on who they are and what represents them and it's strange how conflict makes people search for an identity which often leads them to question their faith more deeply. This was so apparent in all three places. Maybe conflict is 'allowed' by God to get people thinking about who they are…? I know that was certainly the case for me when 9/11 happened. I wanted to know more about my own faith, what it represents, and how I, a Muslim woman of secular background and little religious knowledge, may address some of the questions that were being asked of me about 9/11. I threw myself into the pool of knowledge and soaked up everything I could read – particularly all the negative literature – and then questioned my religious leadership.

Today, I am a better Muslim because I am a thinking Muslim, so I guess 'conflicts' can also have a positive impact on communities too. People in Zanzibar, South Africa and Sri Lanka are working hard to come to terms with their new challenges but without forgetting who they are. This is because their culture is the gelling agent that keeps them together.

'It take more than a horrifying transatlantic voyage chained in the filthy hold of a slave ship to erase someone's culture.' – Maya Angelou

Yours, Anjum

Thursday 1 December

Dear Jonny,

It's the first day of December and your Advent calendar begins. I know, there ought to be a way of making the shops understand that Advent begins with the first of four Sundays before Christmas – but that's another story! As you munch whatever mummy has put in the first drawer of the wooden Advent train that I brought back from Braunschweig in Germany, I'd like to take you straight to a story that moved me more than almost anything else I've experienced in my travels.

In Lahore we were looked after by the Bishop of Raiwind. He is a tremendously energetic and enterprising man, and oversaw the building of the beautiful Cathedral of the Praying Hands – such a lovely dedication for a cathedral! Alongside the cathedral is a school, as well as several projects like clothing sales aimed at assisting girls who've been sold into prostitution.

On our first night we met a group of youth workers. The following morning we discovered that two of them had been asked by the bishop to look after us.

At the end of a long day, one of them, Eugene, sat opposite me as we relaxed in chairs outside the cathedral guest house. Suddenly he burst into tears.

It was completely unexpected.

Eugene had been animated all day. He'd been laughing and joking. He was clearly proud to show us around his city. He was, incidentally, a musician which meant that the two of us had much to talk about. Eugene couldn't read musical notation so he'd asked me to help him find a way to learn. Yet, now, he was in tears.

I've learned as a priest never to rush in when this happens and never to ask what's wrong, which is just about the dumbest question there is. Instead, I found him some tissues and just sat with him until he began to speak.

He said, 'Two weeks ago my girlfriend called to say she wanted to see me. So we arranged to meet, and she told me that her parents had come that day to explain they'd found her a husband. She's Muslim. Ever since we'd been going out, we'd spoken about the fact that our religious identity could be a problem. Not because our religions are against each other – nothing of that sort – but because, well, culturally, it just won't work.'

Eugene kept breaking down as he spoke. But he also kept smiling in a composed, dignified way – something about which I only really reflected afterwards. It was then that I realised the strength and depth of his faith, the strength and depth of his love for his girlfriend and for God.

'What she told me,' he continued, 'of course brought all our discussions to a head. What were we to do? We thought about eloping. Running away. Going to another country. Seeking asylum. A fresh start. A new life. But this would cut us off from our families for ever. I knew we couldn't do it because I kept thinking of my mother. We'd be safe in Holland or wherever. But leaving would put her in danger. Indeed, it's pretty certain she'd be killed as a result, for the shame that I'd brought on their family by 'taking' their daughter from them. That's how they'd see it. So

I said goodbye to the love of my life. I expressed my hope that she'd find happiness and love in her marriage. It broke my heart to do it. But what choice did I have?'

As I write this to you the tears are pouring down my face because I've rarely ever encountered a person of such insight and dignity, of such compassion and love. I looked into his eyes and I saw what we're all encouraged to see in our neighbours: the face of Jesus, the one who gave up his life out of love for others.

I'm not sure I could have done it. I'm not sure I could have been like Eugene. I don't think I'm that selfless.

Of course, inside of me, there's anger as well as the emotion that causes tears – they are all mixed up, I guess. Anger at a culture of honour and shame which has nothing to do with the faith of Islam that I know – since when I look into Anjum's face, for example, I see the faith she lives to be one of extraordinary goodness and kindness.

And yet ...
Lord Jesus,
sometimes words fail
and you just have to take my emotions instead!
Be with all those in the world like Eugene
whose lives are torn apart
by people who simply
do not know what they are doing.
Forgive us when in following our faith
we behave like those who put you on the cross
and inflict a cross on others.
With love, Daddy

Dear Chris,

I have often wondered about the story of Romeo and Juliet, giving up their lives in this world to be together in another world, where love transcends all other values.

I was reminded of Romeo and Juliet as I listened to the young Christian man telling his story about his pain at parting from the love of his life, a Muslim girl. Like you Chris, I am not sure I could have been as brave as this young couple who gave up their love for higher values, both following their own faith traditions.

The young Christian man had insight not only into his own faith, but that of his girlfriend too, for he knew that the future would be fraught with difficulties. Sadly, there are more questions than answers. Or, maybe, we are asking the wrong questions... Perhaps God has plans for these two in a way that we cannot understand.

'Look for the answer inside your question.' — Rumi

Yours, Anjum

Friday 2 December

Dear Jonny,

You're probably thinking about yesterday, 'Okay, that was a story true enough, but did it have to be such a hard one to hear, such a sad one to think about?'

But, as you know, Christmas is not tinsel-lined for a lot of people. It can actually – at least where we live – be the time when more marriages break down, more people commit suicide and more people run away from home than at any other time of the year.

I suppose that's because a lot of people feel left out from the oneness about which I wrote at the start of these letters. Somehow – and I think he knew this was through the grace and power of God – Eugene had held on to the sense that, not just the body of Christ, but his whole community, for all its fractures and brokenness, was the force that could keep him going. I hope that whatever life throws at you you'll find that to be true too.

In the so called first world, in which you and I live – I don't like that name because first suggests best when really, in this case, it means financially wealthiest – we try to find ways to make life easier and easier for us. Not all of this is in any way bad. When my grandfather was growing up in the early years of the twentieth century one of his brothers fell out of an apple tree, hurt his leg badly, suffered from septicaemia and died. I remember seeing my grandad once weeping as he tidied his brother's grave. The only other time I ever saw him cry was when my grandmother – his wife – died. The septicaemia could easily have been cured now by antibiotics. They didn't exist then.

The free health care we enjoy in the United Kingdom is an amazing thing.

However, other ways by which we suppose that we make things easier for ourselves are not so good. We seem to think that the more we own the better we will feel.

Yet, if we return to Luke's good news in chapter 1: 26-38, and listen as he introduces the next part of the diptych – the other side of the painting as it were – we learn that discovering what it means to be human comes at a price. It costs. It requires that we stop thinking selfishly and think, instead, as Eugene did, as selflessly as we can.

The angel Gabriel appears. Yet, not in Jerusalem, that most important city of all. Rather, the angel appears in Nazareth in Galilee, in a place where no one feels that they influence what goes on at the centre of things.

When Mary receives the news that she'll give birth to a baby boy who will be the Son of the Most High – indeed, Son of God – the words she uses are similar to those of Zechariah. You'll remember that he said, 'How will I know that this is so? For I am an old man and my wife is getting on in years.' You'll also recall that as a consequence of this question Zechariah was struck dumb. But when Mary says in reply, 'How will this be, since I have no knowledge of a man?' she isn't similarly struck dumb but reassured by Gabriel.

Perhaps Gabriel was just having an off day when he was sent to Zechariah. Perhaps Luke was trying to make a point about insiders and outsiders. The insiders who should recognise and believe an angel when they've seen one tend not to. This is a warning to religious folk not to get so sucked into the minutiae of their faith systems that they miss the message. Whereas, a supposed outsider like Mary who is young, vulnerable, and knows little of the details of faith does, in fact, get it. Surely the truth is that Gabriel saw in Mary's eyes belief and in Zechariah's unbelief? When thinking about this I am reminded of Eugene's eyes which were full of an extraordinary, translucent faith in God.

It's such eyes full of love and faith that Anjum and I have so often seen in our journeys. We have seen this especially in those who wait on God amid situations of great pain or suffering. This makes their 'yes' to God all the more remarkable. Tomorrow, I want to write to you about one of them in particular.

For now, I'm ending with a prayer of thanks for those like Mary and Eugene whose 'yes' to God costs them dearly:

Life-giving God,
you call each of us to follow in your way
and to discover the truth of your love.
We thank you for the example of all
in whose eyes we see the yes
you desire from each of us
especially when this so often costs time
and leads to suffering and, even, great pain.
Help them and each of us to know
that the cross is never the end of the story
but only the beginning of your new work of recreation.

With love, Daddy

Dear Chris,

This piece made me think about Eid. I was about ten years old when I arrived in the UK. When I saw the buildings blackened by coal fires, cloudy weather and short days, I used to cry and wanted to go back to Pakistan. This was made worse when we had our religious celebrations like Eid! My childhood was spent with extended family members in Pakistan and in the UK I was alone with my parents and two younger sisters. Our school had no idea what Eid was and that feeling of loneliness has never left me. I can relate to those people who feel so lonely at Christmas and I understand how some may feel so dejected that they may wish to commit suicide. That's just so sad! For me, Christmas was never meant to be about 'presents'. It is about listening to what Christians believe about Mary/Mariam and Jesus. Christmas is about the stories that are related around Jesus' birth and how he came to convey the message about the oneness of God.

Yes, you are right Chris. We must 'not get sucked into the minutiae' about our faith that we lose sight of the message. This is happening in our world today as we see religious extremism on the rise. Both Mary and Zechariah are given messages which are difficult to believe. Both question the messenger. Nevertheless, both accept God's decision. That is what we call faith, I guess!

> *'Once the seed of faith takes root, it cannot be blown away, even by the strongest wind, now that's a blessing.' – Rumi*

Yours, Anjum

Saturday 3 December

Dear Jonny,

In Eugene's story I have written about the cost of being a follower of Jesus. Saying 'yes' to God, like Mary and Eugene, is costly. But perhaps in emphasising the cost I am in danger of making it all sound too foreboding...

So, in this letter, let me tell you the story of a remarkable trio of people.

Salim Mohammed is without doubt one of the most remarkable people anyone could meet. Separated from his family at an early age, he grew up in a Muslim children's home, in a place called Eastleigh in Nairobi, in Kenya, under the care of a woman called Mama Fatuma. She was tough. From her, Salim learned a huge amount that one sees in the way he has chosen to live his own life. A devout Muslim, but one who attended the Roman Catholic church opposite the Mama Fatuma children's home, Salim left school with no qualifications. Instead, he left with what's sometimes called 'a degree in people'. In other words, he really understood what makes people tick. He may have been poor in material terms. He may have lacked formal education. Yet, he was rich in qualities which can't be gained from wealth or formal education. He soon recognised that the youngsters of

Eastleigh and Mathare, the district next door, needed creativity in their lives. They needed the framework Mama Fatuma had given him. Football, he knew, could be an agent of transformation – it could bring youngsters together and help them make friends. So, he set about organising teams – a league – which combined football with community action. You got to play football if you came to clean up the community on the 'Thrash the Trash' events he organised.

When he took me to Mama Fatuma's home he also took me to the side street next to it. This street was a place where people threw their carrier bags of rubbish. I walked with him on this stinking mound of soiled nappies, rotting food cans and human waste. Yes, there were piles of that too, because people lived on this rubbish heap. They slept there, sought food there and made a fire there to keep warm at night.

As Salim's community activism progressed and he made a name for himself, he made enemies too. For those who tell the truth – people like John the Baptist and Jesus – are bound to make a few enemies. The truth is too uncomfortable for some people, because it makes them question that they are up to. Most people trusted Salim. When he moved to Kibera – which is the rubbish tip of Nairobi and the largest slum community in the whole of Africa – people trusted his work enough to let him attempt something similar there. This was despite Salim coming from a different tribe to the people of Kibera.

Rye Barcott is another of those people whom you meet and never forget. I first met him when the BBC sent me as part of the team that covered Barack Obama becoming the new president of the United States of America in 2009.

I met Rye because another friend of ours, Jonathan Reiber, was part of a group of young people who were all interested in foreign policy and security issues. They had assembled for a conference designed to coincide with Barack Obama taking office as president. I was really impressed by this young, energetic marine who'd served as a counter-insurgency officer in Afghanistan and Iraq.

As he told me his story I didn't know whether we would meet again. But I somehow had a feeling we would.

He'd studied at the University of North Carolina. His mum was an anthropologist – that's someone who studies the way groups of people live, the customs, frameworks and traditions they share. His dad had served in Vietnam as a marine – all of which goes a long way to explaining who he himself is. He knew he'd be a marine. However, he wanted to go and find out what it was like to live in the very sort of community which gave rise to the insurgencies he would be trained to counter. So, he learned kishSwahili, the language that many Kenyans speak, and he set out to live in Kibera for a summer.

This was, in a way, madness! As a white person he would be pretty much in a minority of one in Kibera. He would stand out. It was a dangerous place. Nevertheless, he was determined to go because he wanted to do what that greatest of all men in the twentieth century, Nelson Mandela, encouraged people to do: to stand in each other's shoes. In other words, to get inside a culture, a place, a people – even a religious framework – that is not your own and really get to know that it feels like. Mandela learned all about the history of the people who imprisoned him for twenty-seven years, the Afrikaners. He could talk about all their most famous battles and their heroes. This meant that when he was released so that talks could begin to create a South Africa that didn't divide people on the basis of the colour of their skin, Mandela could win the trust of those with whom he was talking because he knew the things that mattered most to them in their history.

I haven't finished Salim and Rye's story — and I haven't even introduced the third person in it! But that's enough for today. It'll be good to continue it tomorrow which is a Sunday, a day when we're always encouraged to celebrate what's best in life.

Lord Jesus,
you sometimes put the most unlikely people together
from different cultures, ethnicities and faith traditions
so that they can do your work
and build your kingdom:
help us to see when this is happening
and to join in.
With love, Daddy

Dear Chris,

Salim Mohammed and Rye Barcott are remarkable people who are living out their faith in ways which Jesus and Mohammad would surely approve. Both Jesus and Muhammad suffered for their message. Yet, both worked with those who were in need — the lepers, the troubled, the poor, the wanting and the downtrodden. I often think about our journey together, Chris, and what is it that binds us together? I guess it has to be our understanding of what it means to be human. Could Salim and Rye have connected if they had not tried to understand each other as human beings? Both of these young men came from very different backgrounds, economically, socially and politically. Yet, it was their drive for justice and the courage to have difficult conversations that narrowed their differences.

I guess that is exactly what you and I have been doing for the past 10 years, creating an atmosphere where people can feel comfortable enough to ask the complex questions.

And, you are right: it takes madness to put one's head above the parapet and only then is the unachievable achieved! Salim and Rye are on a journey and I pray that they will continue with their much needed work for the most needy.

'If you wish mercy, show mercy to the weak.' – Rumi

Yours, Anjum

Sunday 4 December

Dear Jonny,

     I wrote yesterday that Sunday is a day when we celebrate all that's best in life. What is best about life? What makes life exciting and rich? As I think about this I'm reminded of a man I know in Cape Town. He drove children from the townships to schools. Every day when you asked him how he was he'd say, 'I'm rich!' I think he knew he was rich in the gifts that counted - the gifts of the Spirit that God gives to serve others. Surely the best thing in life is that we have the chance to serve others – to love and be loved?

     This is what Rye Barcott began to recognise when he spent that summer in Kibera, living in a shack and meeting people in the community.

     It takes courage, or madness, to spend time doing what Rye did. Sometimes he knew he was being followed because he was the *Mzungu* – the white man. And to many Kiberans, white means wealthy. I felt the same when I spent some nights there too. I caused amusement by wearing a red t-shirt which said in Kiswahili, 'I'm a *Mzungu* ... get over it'. Sadly I lost the t-shirt somewhere, though your mother wasn't so sad about that!

The longer Rye stayed the more trust he built, and the closer he got to the heart of a community in which people pay rent to slum landlords. They were paying rent to people who aren't legally meant to charge rent at all, because the whole of Kibera doesn't legally exist! The land is actually owned by the city of Nairobi. No-one has rented out this land to build anything, but after a long struggle some land was released for Salim and Rye and a woman called Tabitha Festo who wanted to build a clinic there. Sadly, Tabitha isn't alive to be part of this now.

Rye met Salim in a way that at first didn't seem promising. Salim was busy doing his football and community work. It had grown considerably. Everyone acknowledged that it was some of the most sustainable work in the slum. He was well used to rich foreigners drifting in and out, handing him money, taking photographs, showing some interest and then disappearing onto the next venue for poverty tourism.

When Rye pitched up at his office wanting to do some work, Salim must have thought, 'Well, here we go again!' They talked about possibilities. Salim wasn't going to put energy into something about which he was unsure. He'd just wait and see if this *Mzungu* actually came back.

It was at this point that Rye met Tabitha Festo and heard her story.

He'd been very careful not to give people money whilst he was there. But when he discovered that what Tabitha most wanted was to buy vegetables to sell them for a profit, so that a clinic could be built in Kibera, he gave her the $26 that would start it all off. He thought nothing of this really. But the next time he came back to Kibera he spotted a shack on the front of which had been painted the words Rye Barcott Clinic. He's a modest guy and was embarrassed by this. Nevertheless, he was of course delighted that Tabitha's venture had been successful.

It was then that he sought out Salim again. But I'll have to finish the story in the next letter and leave you with this prayer to think about as you enjoy the Lord's Day:

> Risen Lord,
> this is your day
> the day when new things happen
> the day when we are all made rich
> in the love feast which is the Eucharist.
> A circle of bread is all that we receive
> but it's all that we need
> to begin to build your kingdom.
> Give us the imagination to do this
> now, not next week
> to offer whatever we can
> the smile, the helping hand
> that actually begins to change the whole world.

With love, Daddy

Dear Chris,

Your story about Salim and Rye reminds me of something that happened to me in India. I had gone there with some friends to open a school and one evening a young woman came to see me where I was staying. She burst into tears. She told me that she had four children and her husband had taken another wife. She had been left with the children on her own. She had no income and she asked if I could help her in any way. You see, I too thought of giving her some money, just like Rye did to Tabitha Festo. However, I was worried about how she would survive tomorrow when she had spent the money. So I asked her to come back the following day with an idea for something that she would like to do to generate income for herself and her children. The following day she was there waiting for me as I was leaving for the school. She walked with me to the school and told me that she always wanted to sell bracelets. Bracelets weren't really what I'd envisaged! Anyway, I asked her to explain. She said that there isn't a single shop in her little village that sells bracelets, and all women, whatever their faith, buy bracelets for weddings, Eid, Holi, Diwali, Basant, Christmas and much more! Now, I had not thought of that! So we decided to go to the nearest town and buy bracelets worth £70.00.

The next day she had set up a little stall in her front room with many colourful bracelets and I was pleasantly surprised to see a few women buying and gazing at the merchandise.

I guess we must learn to listen to those who know what troubles them, and help them understand their issues in their own contexts. Just as Salim was, and is, providing local knowledge to Rye to understand the communities of Kibera!

'Not the ones speaking the same language, but the ones sharing the same feeling understand each other.' — Rumi

Yours, Anjum

Monday 5 December

Dear Jonny,

When Salim and Rye came together the second time that Rye visited Kibera, things were different. Salim knew that Rye was serious – he had come back – and Rye knew that Salim was the person who was the key to the realisation of a dream.

Rye had thought a lot about his time in Kibera. He didn't want just to leave as an observer. He'd already put down some roots of friendship and, through his small gift to Tabitha, he'd become a partner in something that was growing.

He too, like Salim, could see that sports and grassroots activism was one way to turn around lives that could so easily become the seeds of deep tension and unhappiness, between communities and even within them. Somehow Tabitha, Salim and Rye had said 'yes' to something bigger than themselves. From their different faith perspectives, they'd seen what we call a 'common good' and a 'common goal', which was the building up of the community. It was time for it to come together. This is how Carolina for Kibera, one of the best Non-Governmental Organisations (NGOs) I know in the world, was born.

I haven't the space to tell the story in full here. I've already taken up the best part of three letters with it. You can read more about it in the amazing book that Rye himself wrote: *It happened on the way to war: a marine's path to peace.* What I've told you is just some of what Rye and Salim have said to Anjum and me.

The programmes grew. The community came together. Tabitha's clinic went from a shack to the only purpose-built clinic in Kibera. But it's sad that such a wonderful gift to the community is now a memorial to the person who worked hard to get things going: Tabitha died as a result of HIV, a virus that kills your immune system, the system in your body that helps you fight disease. The clinic is no longer the Rye Barcott Clinic, but the Tabitha Festo Clinic. It's a small glimmer of hope, a diamond in the dust. But it's a glimmer nonetheless!

In Advent, that's one of the themes on which we reflect. It's always better to light a candle than to curse the darkness. Of course, in Western Europe where we live, the days are short, the darkness is long, and the idea of a tiny light growing into the presence of the light of the world works well. That's because so much Christmas symbolism was developed in our part of the world.

But, in sub-Saharan Africa, where spring has turned to summer and the days are long, this symbolism doesn't work so easily. In South Africa people often think about the blossoming rose as the symbol for Advent – the rose that has the thorns and hints of the suffering which will be part and parcel of God's experience of being human.

However we picture what happens in Advent, there's something cumulative about it. It's like an energetic movement that grows and can't be stopped.

Lord Jesus,
you have set the flame of your light in me
and you have entrusted within me the gift of love:

help me to send out the tiny ripples of hope
that are needed in home, community, country and world.
Use them to build the current of change
that reveals the glory of your kingdom.

With love, Daddy

Dear Chris,

This letter is very much about creating relationships, and Salim and Rye did exactly that after, no doubt, much self-deliberation and soul-searching. How else could they have realised their dream of bringing some hope to one of the largest slums in Nairobi? What is so amazing about these two people is their love for those who are in great difficulty. Both of these young men have transcended their differences and are steadfast in their vision of bringing some stability and hope to those who desperately need it. Their story makes me wonder if we people of different faiths need to work together on common issues to bring our communities closer to each other... Salim and Rye compel us to think beyond the ordinary! They make us challenge our own limitations. They also make me wonder if we need to challenge our own gremlins first...

'And you, when will you begin your long journey into yourself?' — Rumi

Yours, Anjum

Tuesday 6 December

Dear Jonny,

Margaret Meads, who was a famous anthropologist, once said this: 'Never doubt that a small group of thoughtful, committed citizens can change the world. Indeed, it's the only thing that ever has.'

What brings people together is usually circumstance or connections of identity, be these family, political, social, religious, cultural, national or whatever. The word religion comes, for instance, from a Latin word which means to bind. Hence it suggests that followers of a religion are bound or joined together by tradition, heritage and a common hope.

In Luke's Gospel story leading to Christmas, circumstance and identity collide. Luke brings together the two pictures that he's painted in a meeting of two of the characters he's introduced. Zecharaiah was the one who spoke to the angel. But he was struck dumb because of his unbelief. So, he wouldn't be good for a meeting with Mary, the other person to whom Gabriel spoke. Added to which it makes much better sense for the two women who are pregnant to be brought together. They are – as we've already been told – related. So, they are bound by ties of family, by the circumstance in which they find themselves – they're both expecting babies – and by the similarities and differences of the roles that their respective sons are to play. John will be great. Jesus will be great and Son of the most High. John will prepare God's people for something new. Jesus will actually rule them. John's role is preparatory. The Kingdom Jesus brings will never end. John is a prophet, Jesus is Son of God. John is Spirit-filled, but the overshadowing that sees Jesus born of the Spirit makes him the Holy One. These are all intentional contrasts. They amplify what was mentioned in an earlier letter when I suggested Zechariah and Elizabeth were insiders and city dwellers, relatively well-to-do religious types in the know, whereas Mary is a village peasant girl, an outsider, far from the realities of religious power and influence.

This happens in families. From the same parents can come children who end up in very different places, doing very different things, with very different world views. Maybe they marry someone of a different religion, political persuasion, nationality or culture. They might live in a place which changes their accent. When your elder brothers were in Blackburn, where you were born, they inevitably spoke with Lancashire accents at school. At home, they tended to speak in a less markedly Lancastrian way because your mother and I were brought up in southern cities, me with the West Country accent whose Rs you love to tease me about, your mother in north London.

All these differences matter. They create identity and belonging. You yourself had a Lancashire accent for the first few years of your life. Blackburn was where you were born. Your elder brother hopes that, like him, you'll always be a Blackburn Rovers supporter. He adopted them as his team – but you were born into the community where they are kings!

So, these things mark us out as coming from a particular place and community. They are called identity markers in fact. They point to who we are.

But when Elizabeth and Mary come together, as much as one is a townie and the other a villager, one an elderly religious, the other but the slip of a girl, those things fade into the background. What Luke makes very clear is the fact that their circumstances are the same. They are both pregnant. They have something in common: they have something to share, something to be happy about and, perhaps, something a little fearful too. But this is something that causes the babe in Elizabeth's womb to jump – as sometimes you did in mummy's tummy when you were growing during her pregnancy.

The manuscript versions of Luke's Gospel don't agree as to who sings the song. Some suggest that it's Elizabeth – and this makes perfect sense because, as Luke has been at pains to show us, the old religious world needs to wake up and change. And, the leaping baby is a sign of this as Elizabeth sees Mary and the challenging newness her child will bring. Tradition has tended to say that this is Mary's song, and the church has used the Latin title *Magnificat* for this song that is usually sung during evening worship. It does make sense for Mary to be singing it, but I myself wonder if it makes as much sense as this being Elizabeth's song. However, it's not something I'd get into a fight about!

What's really important is that when it's sung it brings together the existing and the emerging world's – I think that's better than saying old and new, not least because old can often be made to sound outworn and new the thing to have. However, Luke's point is that both tradition and revolution are needed. When they come together – as was the case in the story of Rye, Salim and Tabitha, for instance – something worth singing about often emerges.

One of the issues that Anjum and I have noticed in almost every community we've visited is the struggle of people to embrace both the existing and the emerging in a way that allows for real conversation and dialogue between the two.

It happens here in this meeting of Elizabeth and Mary. Tomorrow, we'll need to think more about the song that emerges as a result.

For now, let's give thanks for the way that God so often brings people together in unexpected ways:

God of circumstance and culture
of family and community
of nation and language
you bring together a Mandela and De Klerk
a Rabin and Arafat
a Paisley and Adams
and in all these ways you do good:
use us in a similar way
to stand in each other's shoes
and to bring healing and hope
as you give us your renewing harmony
in which all may find the notes
to sing of your unending love.

With love, Daddy

Dear Chris,

Yes, we are all connected to each other. Either through our family ties, or religious and cultural ties, or even through our support for a particular football team! There is an invisible thread that binds us together. In my tradition, we Muslims also believe that we belong to one big family under the banner of 'there is no god but God, Muhammad is the Messenger of God.' These few words give us an identity which transcends all other identities. I recognise the story of Zechariah / Mary and Elizabeth, who are all acknowledged in our faith too. But I guess the stories are slightly different, which is to be expected to a certain degree. I suppose we have many identities and we are linked to each other in so many ways.

Nevertheless, should there be one identity that would and does transcend all others? Zechariah / Mary / Elizabeth belonged to different set-ups, but their family identity was stronger than their economic identity, and their religious identity was stronger than all other identities. Some are, as you say, 'outsiders' and some 'insiders' — but what is it that connects them together as one? I think it has to be their faith! In difficult times, it is this identity that matters the most as this connects all those who have multiple other identities under one umbrella. In my case, the Ummah is one big family with outsiders and insiders as one. However, sadly, when one does not communicate or have conversations it is very difficult to have such cohesion.

You are right, Chris — the common thread running through all the people we met was a struggle to come to terms with the challenges they face on a daily basis. They face their challenges by talking to each other, through conversations and dialogues with the 'other.' How many times did we hear the phrase, 'We need to talk to each other?'

'In true dialogue both sides are willing to change.' — Nhat Hanh

Yours, Anjum

Wednesday 7 December

Dear Jonny,

You'll remember that we thought yesterday about the meeting between Elizabeth and Mary. Also, yesterday's prayer reminded us of leaders who've come together to overcome their differences. So, you see, fighting and dispute don't have to be the inevitable outcome when people come together representing different generations or cultures or religious convictions.

One of the countries where this most happened is the one to which we took your old eldest brother when he was four months old. It is also the country where your immediately older brother was born.

In the 1980s, when I was a student, South Africa was in chaos. I was an anti-apartheid activist and it was exciting to see the system of apartheid falling apart. Apartheid had set out to have people of different colours living and being educated separately. When Anjum and I were in Cape Town on our recent visit, the present dean of the cathedral where I worked, Michael Weeder, reflected with us on what life was actually like then.

The South African economy was crumbling. The apartheid government had categorised people into four main groups and put them in the following order of importance: Whites, Indians,

Coloureds and Blacks. But this system was disintegrating for a combination of reasons. It was built on a belief that the black population would grow at a certain level since the policy was formalised in 1948, yet growth had far outstripped those levels. Consequently, the numbers of black people being employed in the cities of South Africa was at a much greater density than envisaged. Also, it was not possible to have the control of movement of South Africans that had been planned. This, in turn, placed a strain on resources and also meant that the gap between whites and the rest, purely in terms of wealth, was widening at an alarming rate. Added to which, there was the amazing resistance to the system from within the Indian, Coloured and Black communities and the heavy pressure of the anti-apartheid movement from outside South Africa. Literally millions of us demonstrated against Nelson Mandela's continued imprisonment, the detaining of countless people without trial, and deaths in detention – to name but a few examples of the issues about which we protested.

Dean Weeder reminded us that as a result of all of this, and the banning of most opposition political parties from the 1960s, a terrific responsibility of joint leadership fell on faith communities. At this time, the United Democratic Front was born as a movement rather than a party to avoid being banned. It brought all faiths together and Dean Weeder himself played an important role in it. If Archbishop Desmond Tutu called a 'prayer service' at what became known as the people's cathedral – that's St George's Cathedral in Cape Town – then everyone came: Baha'i, Buddhist, Christian, Hindu, Jain, Jewish, Muslim, Zoroastrian, and more. They all came because circumstance, again, had given them a commonality that they could share: they were against apartheid and for multi-racial democracy.

Their common song was really the one that Mary sang: scatter the arrogant, pull down the mighty, send the rich away empty-handed; whilst exalting the lowly, filling the hungry and taking the hands of people to give them the freedom of a new world order. Later, in chapter 6 of Luke's Gospel, we see that these things are at the heart of what Christians call the Beatitudes, the central teaching of Jesus which shows who's pulled down and who's lifted up in this new Kingdom of justice and joy.

Dean Weeder talked movingly with us about how this song emerged into what, in 1994, was called the new South Africa. Or, as Archbishop Tutu depicted it, the 'rainbow people of God'. We confirmed what we'd heard from him in countless conversations and group meetings we had across Cape Town. But he also said something very telling which was that the inter-religious energy of those times had not been translated into a sustained commitment to live and work together in the new South Africa. The result of this failure to embrace a bigger version and vision of the Kingdom of God was seen in a retreat into each faith's own ghetto – a movement back into the safe world of Zechariah and Elizabeth before they were challenged by God; rather than the more risky, on the edge, at the margins world of communal activism.

In part, this was inevitable of course. It's rare that people are able to sustain the sort of momentum that's needed. A previous dean, Colin Jones, who was the dean at the height of the struggle in the 1980s, used to say 'we fought for freedom and all we ended up with was democracy.' There is truth in this. Freedom has to be expressed in institutions, but these institutions themselves may sometimes be as shackling as the ones they replaced. I know in relation to this that I upset some of my South African friends when I wrote a letter to *Cape Times* challenging the faith communities to come out of their ghettoes and respond to the manifest injustices still being experienced across faith and ethnic divides. Someone said that they felt I had betrayed the struggle in which I played only a small but committed part. But I was angry at the faith

communities for their failure to speak out when members of the
ruling party, the African National Congress, decided that the only
way to address issues of public service delivery (and the failure
to empty toilets more regularly and address long-term issues of
sewerage) was to come to the steps of the Provincial Buildings
in Cape Town and pour faeces all over them. As I wrote angrily,
using a word I hope you won't be using in a hurry, 'I didn't chain
myself to South Africa House in London, and endure a beating
and arrest by the police of my own nation, so that people in the
new South Africa could throw shit around the place.' Of course,
what happened to me was nothing compared to what millions
of South Africans endured day by day during apartheid. But if
you remember from an earlier letter, where I talked about the
cost of following a faith and suggested that it brings us each a
cross to carry as Christians, then you'll perhaps understand why
I've found it very difficult to stomach the emergence of a new
South Africa in which such bad behaviour is a feature. A big part
of caring, of being passionate and compassionate is a desire to
see things be better, not the same.

So you see there are real needs and challenges for faith
communities to work together. In the next letter, I want to write
a bit more about what has happened in this regard in Eastleigh,
a suburb of Nairobi in Kenya.

> Ever-powerful God
> you scatter the arrogant
> pull down the mighty
> send the rich away empty-handed
> while exalting the lowly
> filling the hungry with good things
> and taking the hands of your people
> to give them their freedom:

help us to realise

that this isn't just your task

it's ours right now.

With love, Daddy

Dear Chris,

Having disagreements is natural — how such disagreement pans out is more important. Not all disagreements have to have hostile conclusions but this would depend on the leadership offered. A good leader would need to bring all the different factions to a point on their journey where their individual differences will have to take secondary place. The many tribes in South Africa and many people from different ethnic backgrounds had to be 'led' to overcome their differences, so that they could see the bigger picture. We see this quality in the prophets and the messengers of God. In recent times we have had the giants like Nelson Mandela and Mahatma Gandhi, as well as, among the living, Archbishop Emeritus Desmond Tutu and the present Dean of Cape Town, who create space for people to come together for a common purpose: one purpose, one aim, one objective and, more importantly, one voice. It takes courage to challenge people and the faith communities need to be challenged, but of course there are consequences. Jesus challenged the establishment and he was castigated. Today, our faith communities have returned to their comfort zones and it will take strong leadership to bring them out of these — hopefully soon, because sitting on the fence simply will not do!

> *'If you are neutral in situations of injustice, you have chosen the side of the oppressor.' — Desmond Tutu*

Yours, Anjum

Thursday 8 December

Dear Jonny,

Little Mogadishu is the place where Salim Mohamed spent his childhood in the Mama Fatuma Children's Home. It's the place where I met a family living on a mound of other people's rubbish. It's also the community where Anjum and I spent time giving several workshops. At the end of one of these I found myself alone with a person who turned out to be a member of the Al Shabaab terrorist network. Perhaps I'll tell you about that in a later letter!

So far I've referred to it as Eastleigh, using the name that the British colonisers gave it and which it still bears. Eastleigh is actually a place in Southampton in Hampshire in England. A regiment from Hampshire's Eastleigh went out to Nairobi and they used a name which reminded them of life 'back home'. This sense of 'back home' has all sorts of consequences for life among the people whose territory or country is being taken over. For one thing, it gives it an identity which belongs more to the colonisers than the colonised. For another, it forces an identity on people which isn't theirs and it can end up destroying the local character of the community – its language, customs and history. It can make people inhabit a history not their own. This has profound consequences.

But why, you may be wondering is Eastleigh now known as Little Mogadishu?

The original Mogadishu, like the original Eastleigh, is not in Kenya but in Somalia. It's a famous coastal town. The reason for Eastleigh now being known as Little Mogadishu is because over the last fifty years a district which once had a colonial army barracks and houses for the officers of the British colonial government has now seen a different wave of immigration from Somalia.

Most of the offices of the colonial government were Ken-Indians. In other words, they were immigrants from the Indian subcontinent brought over by the British to build the infrastructure of Kenya – the railway line between Mombasa and Nairobi would be one example – and then to service the administrative needs of the infrastructure they had created. On some of the buildings in Eastleigh you may still see Hindu script, as also a style of building that gives away the identity of the original occupants as Hindus or Muslims from India. You may also see many of the small houses that were built for these colonial civil servants to occupy.

Before independence, much of Kenya's coffee, for instance, was designed almost solely for the British Empire's markets. But since independence, trading with other African countries has become more important, with a particular focus on Somalia. This has brought literally thousands of Somalian traders and business people to Nairobi. It's also seen lower-skilled migrant workers from Somalia follow their more skilled neighbours in the hope of a better life. In the light of the civil war in Somalia of recent years, this influx has accelerated and made the community feel like home from home – only this time not to the British colonisers or the Indian migrants who worked for them, but to Somalians. Hence the title Little Mogadishu.

Before this shift in the composition of the population, Eastleigh contained Hindus, Christians and Muslims. The Hindu and Christian communities remain but are now in a minority, because the majority of the Somalians who have migrated are Muslim.

I know that you're very aware of attitudes about migrants in our own country, not only because you've heard a lot on the news about it but because it affects the life of your own class at school. Almost all the friends you invited to your last birthday party – which was almost every boy in your class as far as I could tell – are migrants of second or first generation. To me the diversity was amazing – wonderful! But from what you've heard you'll also know that when this sort of migration happens, however fast or slow its pace, it makes people anxious. The 'host' communities – these may be people who have lived in a place for thousands of years or be fairly recent migrants themselves who have settled in an area – perhaps feel that their identity is being 'swamped'. That was the word that the British Prime Minister recently used to describe the many people in migrant camps in Calais in France who all seem to be trying to come to Britain in the hope of a better life. Many people felt that 'swamped' was a very negative and unhelpful word to use. But I don't want to get fixed on the word itself, rather to acknowledge the perception or feeling behind it: this is that people sense their identity is threatened. They also sense that it will be changed as they suppose they are moving from being the majority to the minority culture or faith in their community.

This is actually some of the background to the story in Luke that we've been following. The Jewish people were an occupied people. They were governed by the Romans and this, too, brought an influx of traders and business people from neighbouring cultures that were felt to threaten Jewish identity.

In Eastleigh, it was amid some of these tensions and complexities that a group of Muslims and Christians decided to come together to assess the real story of its identity. In part, they were trying to test together whether Eastleigh had indeed become Little Mogadishu under the influence of Somalian culture. They no doubt wanted to see what this new identity felt like for the communities who had been there before their Somalian neighbours arrived.

I thought that I would get to that story today but I realised as I was writing that the story of migration is such a complex one. You needed to know some of the background before I could tell you something about the work of the Christian-Muslim Study Centre in Eastleigh which is part of St Paul's University, Limuru, an Anglican university set in the hills just outside of Nairobi. To this we will, I promise, turn after I've told you tomorrow about the two people who are behind it.

> God of so many nations and cultures
> of many faiths and creeds
> you call us to share a common humanity
> with each and every one of our neighbours.
> This often means that we must embrace
> a diversity of views and lifestyles
> of opinions and beliefs
> that can be very confusing.
> Give us patience to listen
> courage to ask questions
> and a spirit of respectfulness
> that will enable us to find the unity in diversity
> which is your life as Trinity.

With love, Daddy

Dear Chris,

Strange how the colonisers have a habit of changing spellings and sometimes totally anglicising the names of places, which may not roll off their tongues so smoothly! I'm reminded of Peking/Beijing or Bombay/ Mumbai, and of course the de-Anglicisation of these cities back to their original spellings/names gives the colonised a sense of ownership and pride.

Sadly, it is not just the change of spellings or change of names of the streets or towns that does the trick. Colonisation has impacted generations and has created an enslaved mindset. Our visit to Eastleigh was an eye opener! For centuries these people lived side by side without any major conflict, until the 'outsiders' came to sow the seeds of discontent.

I think political correctness is killing the desire of many communities to want to speak up and ask the difficult questions. In fact, it was in Nairobi that a Christian woman said to me that this was the first time she felt comfortable enough to ask some difficult questions of a Muslim! How sad is this? One lives next door to a Muslim, but the thought that we may somehow be offending the other causes us to speculate rather than ask the question. But there are always some good people who will raise their heads above the parapet and challenge misconceptions, and we met many in Eastleigh who are desperately trying to create opportunities for conversations.

There is the difficult question of refugees at the moment in our own country and most of the refugees are Muslims who are migrating due to persecution and safety issues. These Muslims are practicing their faith and will therefore impact the public square discourse, keeping faith visible both in private and in public! This, I think, can only be good. However, many secularists would want the Muslims to keep their faith in private. Only time will tell how this pans out in the future.

'The worst thing that colonialism did was to cloud our view of our past.' —
Barack Obama

Yours, Anjum

Friday 9 December

*D*ear Jonny,

Dr Joseph Wandera, who teaches at St Paul's University, Limuru, and Professor Esther Mombo, who until very recently was its Pro Vice-Chancellor, are two people who'd definitely not see themselves as John the Baptist type figures. As a feminist or womanist theologian – that's someone who is keen to ensure that the church doesn't interpret the bible in ways that exclude the perspective of women – Esther would doubtless balk at being associated with an aggressive male role model! But Joseph and Esther are certainly prophetic.

Someone who is a prophet takes a risk in saying what people often do not want to hear. Kenya is a very patriarchal society, where men are always seen to be exercising leadership, or at least they do so over women. Also, there are divisions between Christians and Muslims in Kenya – and it is sad to see some Christians and Muslims talk about each other in ways that do not honour their God-given humanity. In such a context, both Esther and Joseph have been immensely courageous in addressing the key issues. Joseph – who completed his research as a doctor of theology at the University of Cape Town – hasn't fought shy of exploring the difficulties of relations between people of different faiths. With Esther he has sought to model how the two faiths might engage at a deeper level, without avoiding their differences or difficulties, but speak from the heart of their traditions with respect as well as clarity.

You'll remember in our journey through the first two chapters of Luke's Gospel we looked at the moment when Elizabeth and Mary came together. We thought about the song that emerged as a result of that meeting - the song that pointed the way to the heart of the message for which Jesus would live and die. But next in the diptych, Luke must describe the moment when the babies are born.

John the Baptist is first, of course in Luke chapter 2 from verses 57-80.

Luke's focus is not the birth of John. It's the birth of Jesus that's most important.

People expected baby boys to be named after their fathers. So everyone expects this boy to be called Zechariah. Though his father at this point cannot speak, his mother Elizabeth states that he is to be called John. In a patriarchal way, something that Esther would rightly want to challenge, everyone looks to the father to confirm that this is the case! He readily agrees that he should be called John, which means 'God is gracious'.

Biblical names always have significance, and to say that God is gracious means that God is doing a new thing through this baby boy.

Freed from his dumbness, Zechariah goes on to sing a song – which follows the pattern of the traditional Jewish prayer, *berakah*. After months of silence, Zechariah could be forgiven for babbling away in his excitement at now being able to speak – he is the first to experience the freedom through his son's future work about which he sings. But his song is very ordered and of course, like Mary's, refers back to the hymn book of the Bible, the Psalms, as well as containing echoes of moments in Jewish history like the Exodus, for example, when God set people free from slavery. Such moments are times when people experienced the graciousness of God through his direct intervention to bless them.

Just as Joseph and Esther have sought to set Kenyans free from the impact of bad religious dispute on the one hand and male-dominated thinking on the other, so the arrival of John announces that God has come to set people free. This is to happen through the one God provides as Saviour – not John but his relative Jesus who is descended from David. Long ago, God promised this in the prophets. John is the last of them. God is going to save the people of Israel from their enemies and haters. God always promised that his mercy would be shown to his people and that the covenant he made with them would always be remembered and kept.

Given the emphasis on God freeing or liberating his people, some might suppose that the covenant to which Zechariah is referring is the one made through Moses. But Zechariah is very specific. He refers here not to the covenant with Moses rather to that with Abraham (Genesis 22: 17), to which St Paul also makes reference in his letter to the Christians in Galatia (3: 6-18). This is crucial for the message of Jesus that Luke tries to explain. It means that Christians are children of Abraham, since the covenant with Moses was very specifically Jewish. And while Zechariah goes on to use a wonderful image to describe the way in which his son John will point to Jesus – the day star from on high dawning on those who dwell in the darkness – we would perhaps do well to dwell on the significance of this reference to Abraham which might easily be missed. For as the work of Esther Mombo and Joseph Wandera has sought to show, it's not just the Christians and Jews who are children of Abraham, it's the Muslims too, and beyond them, all who are children of God. In the next letter I'll try to describe to you something of how this has been worked out in Eastleigh.

> God of Abraham,
> you are forever the bright star
> dawning on all who dwell
> in darkness:
> help us to know that this star
> is not our possession
> or the treasure of the few
> but blazing light for everyone

With love, Daddy

Dear Chris,

When people raise their heads above the parapet questions are asked and on many occasions the risk-takers are ostracised for speaking up to bring about change in their communities. Dr Wandera and Professor Mombo both have challenged the status quo, and have sent out ripples in the educational and religious communities. Their work reminds me, Chris, of some of the work that you and I have done in Blackburn and beyond in challenging our own faith communities about difficult subjects. Jesus challenged the establishment in his time. In fact, I often wonder what would happen if he walked into the Bank of England today? All the prophets have tried to set people free from the shackles of 'bad religion' and bring them back to worshipping the One God.

Being like the three monkeys – 'hear no evil, do no evil, see no evil' – is not always helpful. By shutting out challenges and difficulties one does not solve the issues. From my faith perspective both Mary/Mariam and Zechariah did not suffer from 'dumbness' but were instructed to keep 'fast' from speaking. Today we need to 'fast' from talking and use the other God-given faculties to understand each other!

> 'Words are a pretext. It is the inner bond that draws one person to another, not words.' — Rumi

Yours, Anjum

Saturday 10 December

Dear Jonny,

On 21 September 2013, unidentified gunmen from the terrorist group Al Shabaab attacked the Westgate Shopping Mall in Nairobi. It's a place full of shops and restaurants and I had had several meals myself there just days before. Across the space of twenty-four hours 67 people were killed, including 4 gunmen, and around 175 people were reported as injured. The attack was seen as revenge for the fact that Kenyan troops had been deployed in what was the homeland for the group, Somalia.

Jilan Shah, a friend whom I interviewed after the attacks during one of Anjum and my visits, lay for about nine hours in one of the stores which the gunmen entered. Hiding between clothes racks, he'd dropped his mobile phone when he'd dived for cover as a shop assistant told people to hit the ground when the shooting began.

A gunman definitely came into the shop since Jilan remembered seeing his shadow and praying that his mobile phone did not go off. Thankfully, the battery was so low that it switched itself off naturally. But he couldn't move to see whether this was the case for fear that he would be shot. He heard some shooting from the gunman and, in fact, a person in the store was shot dead. He was only able to move after about nine hours when police entered the shop to usher out anyone trapped.

It was the background of this terrifying experience and ongoing violence that caused Dr Joseph Wandera and Professor Esther Mombo to suggest a joint exercise for some of the Christian students of St Paul's University and some Muslims living locally in Eastleigh. In small groups, the students and residents of different faiths had sought to map the district and they shared the results with Anjum and me. They had been trying to identify significant buildings in terms of worship and recreation, hospitality and business, commerce and residential accommodation, in a way that would identify key aspects of the district.

One of the features they observed, for instance, was that if you walk from first to twelfth street you really walk from extreme poverty to extreme wealth – from Mama Fatuma's children's home to the offices of some of Somalia's biggest banks. Another feature they observed was the way in which institutions could more closely be linked. There is a Roman Catholic church opposite the children's home in First Street. Salim Mohamed recalls going to that church, partly to steal loose change from the offertory box at the back so that he could buy fruit for the youngest boys at the children's home. The parish priest ignored this because he saw the bigger picture and the poverty of the children. They, in turn, respected him and often went to services, despite the fact that they were Muslims. After the services they not only received some food and a drink but also swept the forecourt to help the priest.

Such narratives were uncovered as the district was mapped and these are crucial. Since there has been no official mapping of the district and also no attempt to record the stories that animate every community – like Salim's linking of the Muslim children's home and the Roman Catholic church – much communal memory is being lost. At the time that Anjum and I were there, the Nairobi City Council had not collected the rubbish for about seven months, partly for fear of ambush by the terrorists they knew were hiding amid the commercial ventures of this sprawling suburb. But when fear takes over and people retreat into their ghettoes new, much less positive, stories take hold. These are stories like the ones we heard in Zanzibar when a UK agency who, as I said before should have known a good deal better, sought to whip up hatred among the Anglican priests about their Muslim brothers and sisters.

We visited a mosque in Eastleigh, for example, next to which a Pentecostal church had set itself up. An enormous structure with seats for around a thousand people, it rarely got more than about a hundred. Nevertheless, with a routine that was sickeningly calculated to irritate, every time the Muslim call to prayer was heard the sound system of this church – its external speakers set up specifically to point at the mosque – blared out worship songs loudly. Members of the Christian-Muslim Centre in Eastleigh have recognised that this has the potential to ignite what is already a tinderbox context, and they have sought to enable dialogue to reduce the potential tensions. The pastor of the church had walked out of one meeting but they were hopeful of getting him back to the table and hopeful too that links with another more moderate church would create some leverage.

Of course, in the face an atrocity like the one at the Westgate Mall, such conversations seem but drops in the ocean. Yet, they are part of a grassroots movement that is gaining ground in other places like Zanzibar where people have lived together peacefully but where local, national and international events see the pendulum of public mood shifting very quickly. People don't now ask questions. They simply react to whatever information is placed before them, however inaccurate it may in fact prove to be. So there's much work to be done and, as we learned in the workshops we held in Eastleigh and at Limuru, there's a critical mass of people beginning to do it.

> Thank you, Lord
> for those who see beyond the instantaneous
> and for whom now is tempered by reflection
> and consideration, not only of the facts
> but of the feelings of neighbour and stranger alike.
> Inspire more to be like them
> to think and pray from the heart
> for the good of all your people.

With love, Daddy

Dear Chris,

Religions need a vehicle to travel on, and culture provides exactly this. Religions would die if they could not work with various cultures. Those who have become literalists tend to fall prey to what we have come to term as radicalisation/fundamentalism and extremism. We are witnessing the resurgence of some very bad religion coupled with some very bad governmental policies which is putting people at risk.

Nairobi witnessed such a tragedy, but we thank God for the likes of Dr Joseph Wandera and Professor Esther Mombo who have taken the initiative to create a safe space at St. Paul's University for people of various faiths to understand each other.

Why should people need safe space for conversation? What has driven them indoors into their own safe places? Fear has been created in both Christian and Muslim communities. We have seen this in Zanzibar and in

Pakistan, where both communities lived in relative peace, even with interfaith marriages, yet today are afraid to speak to one another. People in Eastleigh are working to bring some sense of security to their communities and each faith community has a responsibility to lessen fear of 'the other'. For fear to be obliterated more Wanderas and Mombos are going to be needed to raise their voices for peace!

'Hope is being able to see that there is light despite all of the darkness.' — Archbishop Emeritus Desmond Tutu

Yours, Anjum

Sunday 11 December

Dear Jonny,

There is a wordlessness about a small baby or child that is completely captivating. Once when we were in Colombo, the capital of Sri Lanka, we were walking late one afternoon around the memorial in Independence Square and I realised that I was being followed by a one year old child. Anjum said it was because I was white and, thus, an oddity to the child. Whatever motivated her toddling after me, she was coming to check me out, as they say.

We couldn't exchange words. We didn't share a common language. And the little girl wasn't yet speaking anyway – at least not in words. But we shared smiles and giggles, and her outstretched hand towards mine made for a moment of encounter that was both beautiful and uplifting.

Advent is about a baby. That's its point. We aren't waiting for a turkey. We aren't waiting for Christmas pudding. We're waiting for a baby. But we're also waiting for a moment of complete wordlessness.

Now, as you know well enough by now – because you've listened to many sermons (including some which you've found very boring!) – that's the sort of thing that preachers often say, leaving people baffled as to what they mean.

So, at the risk of being boring let me explain. Yet, let me not use prose. I will use poetry instead.

'The word made flesh made word again.' That's what the poet Edwin Muir once said was the real danger for Christianity, especially in relation to its worship. In Christianity we say that Jesus Christ is the Eternal Word of God. This basically means that God is the calling One – the word or the phrase, if you like – that summons everything into existence. In other words, all that you see around you and you yourself have been uniquely brought into being by God. This Eternal Word becomes human. It takes flesh and bones in a life that is not just full of speech, but full of feeling, full of love!

Too much of Christmas is about words. Some of them are lovely and the music that goes with them is beautiful too. But often they get in the way.

One of the most wonderful priests I knew was a man called John V Taylor, who spent years in Africa writing about the indigenous religion that was there before Christianity or Islam or Judaism came. He used to write a poem each Christmas. Poems, though they use words, do so in a concentrated way as if each syllable is the brush stroke on a painting. He said that after he became a bishop writing poetry was perhaps the only time he could spend really thinking about the coming of Jesus. Here's one of those Christmas poems. I think it's his best and it's simply called *To a Grandchild*:

> Over the swinging parapet of my arm
> your sentinel eyes lean gazing. Hugely alert
> in the pale unfinished clay of your infant face,
> they drink light from this candle on the tree.

Drinking, not pondering, each bright thing you see,
you make it yours without analysis
and, stopping down the aperture of thought
to a fine pinhole, you are filled with flame.
Give me for Christmas, then, your kind of seeing,
not studying candles — angel, manger, star —

but staring as at a portrait, God's I guess,
that shocks and holds the eye, till all my being
gathered, intent and still, as now you are,
breathes out its wonder on a wordless yes.

Give me for Christmas your kind of seeing. Not speaking, seeing! Looking at God come as a baby, just as I looked and smiled at that child in Independence Square. Looking at that child made me realise that deep down we were both connected, neither by a common language nor by a common belief system nor by a common nationality or culture, but by the deepest thing of all: the God who created us and loves us for all eternity.

'The truth that holds us is always greater than the truth to which we hold.' Those are the words of another bishop, John Tinsley, who was bishop of Bristol when I was a chorister at the cathedral. He influenced me more than he would ever know. He was a towering intellect of a man, but he treated me, a small child finding my way in the faith, with more respect than almost any other adult I'd met by then. That respect left a deep impression. It's something I'll never forget. It's the bedrock of human community. It's actually what God showed to each and every one of us by taking our flesh, for as John Tinsley also rightly said, 'God cannot be got into words.'

Lord Jesus,
the world needs the kind of respect you showed
for the whole human race

the world needs the kind of wordlessness
that the gurgling and smiling of a baby show to us.
When we hold new life we know that it represents all life
we know that nothing should ever harm a gift so precious.
Enfold us in this truth again this Christmas and always.

With love, Daddy

Dear Chris,

The child at Independence Square really did not care about the colour, creed or sex of the person to whom she stretched out her hand — she saw humanity in you, Chris. She felt comfortable because children have not 'learned' prejudice at that age! Children have a knack of speaking the truth as they see it. Both you and the little girl did not speak, but your actions spoke volumes. We do not always need words.

Jesus was God's word, so you say. My faith also says that 'God said BE and it was' and it was God's word. The same act is described in different ways, but Jesus remains the centre piece, without him the lost sheep cannot find its way! We seem to have put his words into our books and put our books on the shelves. We speak of Jesus and Muhammad, but we do not walk their talk. We have forgotten how to 'do' Jesus in our everyday life and we certainly do not search for him within ourselves. Rather, we seem to search for him in our shopping malls at Christmas! How sad!

'Maybe Christmas, the Grinch thought, doesn't come from a store.' — Dr Seuss

Yours, Anjum

Monday 12 December

Dear Jonny,

Do you remember quite a way back in these letters when I talked to you about the genealogy with which Matthew begins his telling of the Good News? Since then, we've been following Luke's story and the beautiful diptych that he paints bringing Elizabeth and Mary together.

But if we are to keep the stories running in parallel and reach Christmas we need now to return to Matthew's tale and to the person – apart from the two babies – who most shows the quality of wordlessness about which I spoke in yesterday's letter. This is Joseph who acted as Jesus's father even though he wasn't biologically his father. Matthew ends that family tree saying, 'and Jacob the father of Joseph the husband of Mary, of whom Jesus was born, who is called Messiah.'

There've been, as I spoke about long ago now, a fair few irregularities in the family tree so far. There are, in fact, five mothers who are all misfits: Tamar, who gave birth to illegitimate twins; Rahab, a prostitute; Ruth, a Moabite – and Moabites were enemies of the people of Israel; and Uriah's wife Bathsheba, whom David stole from her husband. Mary comes at the end of this list of mothers but it's not really her who's the misfit. It's Joseph. The question which Matthew wrestles with in the rest of the first chapter of his story (Matthew chapter 1 verses 18 to 25) is about the extent to which Joseph can be seen as Jesus's father.

Mary and Joseph were betrothed, they were engaged to be married, as we would now put it. But before their marriage Mary was found to be pregnant. This wasn't the way things were done. All the villagers would have wondered who had fathered the child. Was it Joseph? Or, had Mary slept with someone else – which would have been in keeping with the list of the mothers Matthew gives earlier in chapter one? But this is not what actually happened, according to Matthew.

Joseph had options here. There was then no paternity testing – no DNA swabs – to prove whose father the child was. The law said that all that was needed for someone to prove that they were the father of a child was to give the child a name. If Joseph had refused to do this, if he'd collected the witnesses he needed, he could have proved Mary's unfaithfulness and had her stoned to death. Sadly, as we know, there are some communities in the world where this happens and where people argue that their religion allows it. Some Muslims, for instance, have been known to stone women to death for sleeping with a man who is not her husband. But the prophet Mohammed, to whom Muslims always add the respectful phrase 'peace be upon him' when they refer to him, said that there always had to be four actual witnesses to an act of what is called 'adultery' before someone could be stoned – this was actually a very clever way of making sure that it could never happen!

But I'm digressing. As you know, I tend to do that quite a lot! So let's get back to Joseph's response to what might easily have seemed to him unfaithfulness. He could have disgraced Mary and had her stoned. Instead, what he planned to do was the least painful of all the options under the law – this was to assemble a few witnesses, say that the marriage was off, without saying the reason, and leave Mary to get on with being a single parent.

For me, this story presses a lot of personal buttons since I was born an illegitimate child, the product of a short relationship between a mother and father who 'gave me up for adoption,' as the phrase goes. Your grandparents, my adoptive parents, really acted like Mary and Joseph since I was not their child biologically. I 'did not grow under my mother's heart but in it,' as a prayer for adopted people runs. Yet, they named me – the key to paternity in Jesus's times – and they cared for me with all the love they could give. Though Jesus was of course born from Mary's womb, how far we can see him as Mary's son in the conventional way is open to dispute. But that, as they say, is like opening Pandora's Box. As your brothers would put it, 'don't go there!'

I've got a little ahead of the story with another tangent. Joseph's original intention to dismiss and abandon Mary may not seem such a good one to us now. However, within the constraints of his times, it was the most generous of the possible solutions available to him. But God had other ideas!

As God broke into the world through an angelic messenger who spoke to Zechariah and Mary, so now, in a dream, God breaks into the unconscious world of a man who is never reported as saying anything anywhere in the Bible at all, but whose actions speak much louder than any words could.

As with the angel's previous appearances, reassurance is offered, 'Do not be afraid.' When John orders his version of the Good News he actually has the very first of his 'I am' sayings of Jesus as, 'I am, be not afraid.' So many people live in fear in the world. So many of the people with whom Anjum and I have spoken have fear in their eyes. I want to tell you about a group of them in the next letter, in fact.

But once fear is conquered – the angel knows this insight – change can begin. Joseph can accept that the child with whom Mary is pregnant is not another man's responsibility but the Holy Spirit's. Remember what I said about the importance of naming the child? Joseph is now told that he will have two names and the clear implication is 'you must give them to him and be his father by taking Mary as your wife.' He will be Jesus – which means 'God saves'. This is the same name as Joshua. So it's a traditional Jewish name that expresses their hope for salvation. Jesus will save the community – not individuals. He will not lead an army but a revolution of the heart, a revolution from within as it were, because when sin and wrongdoing is conquered then the most important war has been won.

The root of the word to save means 'to give space'. Salvation for the Jewish people meant having their own space – a land. But here it means more. Saving people from their sins means creating that space within and between people which enables them to flourish. We are back to that familiar idea that has run through many of these letters: we are one. Acknowledging other people – giving them their space, as we now say – is the only way to achieve real peace.

But Jesus has another name too – and this is as important. He is Emmanuel, God with us. The most distinctive thing about the faith to which you and I belong lies in the claim that God becomes human in Jesus Christ. Our Muslim and Jewish sisters and brothers cannot agree to this claim because for them God is wholly other, he is beyond. I don't want to fall here into one of the traps that I could easily set for myself – and for you – by getting the tone wrong. But I think after the many conversations I've had with Jewish and Muslim friends, some of them with Anjum on our visits, I feel confident to say that Christianity's claim to believe in the God-human we call Jesus is literally a scandal for Judaism and Islam. Scandal is a strong word. But I am using it in what we call an 'objective' not a 'subjective' way. They wouldn't be saying that we are a scandal for believing such a thing. But I do believe they would be scandalised – that means their whole way of looking at things would be skewed and compromised – by what they see as an impossibility.

This latest of my tangents is actually crucial because how people of different faiths have this sort of conversation is critical for the future of the world. In other words, as Christians, how we talk about our beliefs without insulting others', how we enable people to listen and how we ourselves listen to their responses without feeling insulted are all important.

It's a lot for Joseph to take onboard in one dream. But a lot can happen in fact in dreams. Some people dismiss them as fairy stories. But many people in the Western world study them. And, in Africa often people talk of God calling them in a dream. So Martin Luther King, who fought to have black and white Americans treated equally, stood in a very long tradition by beginning his most famous speech with the words 'I have a dream'. Things change when we have dreams. Joseph awakes, says nothing, but takes Mary as his wife. When the child is born Joseph names him Jesus.

Your name Jonathan is an ancient Jewish name. It means 'God has given'. I hope that you will be able to give to everyone you meet what God has given to you of his love and blessings. Perhaps part of the secret for each of us lies in our name?

God of our dreams,
we are each given a name
we are each engraved on the palms of your hands
and with this we receive your blessing and love:
help us to honour your call in us
and to recognise it in neighbour and stranger.

With love, Daddy

Dear Chris,

Genealogies help us to understand those in the Scriptures, although some people get lost and their stories are not followed up. Joseph is not someone that I am familiar with, and he certainly does not get a mention in my Scriptures. Mary, the virgin mother has a whole chapter named after her and she is the only woman mentioned by name in the Qur'an. But once she delivers Jesus, she too disappears from the pages of history in my Scriptures. When Mary is informed that she is to bear a child, she becomes bewildered and asks, 'How can that be, as no man has touched me?' According to Christian texts, Mary was engaged to be married to Joseph and this information would be in the public domain — would her community have speculated about her pregnancy especially as she was to be married to Joseph?

We can all walk into a dark room and touch a different part of the elephant and report our own experience — one story, many interpretations! Why not let Jesus return and explain all — oh! what a day that would be! Until then, we dream of a safe world and work together for one!

'Great dreams of great dreamers are always transcended.' — A P J Abdul Kalam (late President of India)

Yours, Anjum

Tuesday 13 December

*D*ear Jonny,

Yesterday we talked about dreams and the way in which for Joseph the dream that he was given caused him to act outside the confines of his context, with its normal expectations of behaviour. So he and Mary became husband and wife and he named Jesus as his son. However, sometimes – indeed too frequently on the visits that Anjum and I have made – we found that it's the other way round, and the contexts in which people live shatter even the most basic of human dreams.

In Sri Lanka, for instance, we found a subtle sort of shattering of dreams. In that majority Buddhist context existing churches could be restored but planning permission was not given for new ones to be built. This was also true in Zanzibar, where the cathedral – a world heritage site because the high altar was built above the tree to which slaves were chained when they were sold – may be being restored but other churches are crumbling and new ones are not feasible because permission will not be given to build them.

But it's not just an issue about buildings. It's also about people. In Zanzibar, Anjum and I spent a Thursday evening with a group of Christian students from the state university. I'm not going to mention where we met them because that would perhaps put the students and the couple who are supporting them in danger. What I will say is that they were from various Christian denominations and from a number of different African nations. They did not feel comfortable worshiping openly within the university context which is, like the rest of Zanzibar, predominantly Muslim. You may remember from a previous letter that Muslims and Christians have lived on this beautiful island together happily for hundreds of years and that the presentations given by a group from Britain had caused more anxiety among Christians about their Muslim neighbours. But it would, nonetheless, be fair to say that some Muslims who do not represent the best of Islam have stirred up increasing hatred of what is called 'the other', especially among young people. This, of course, means hatred of those who are not Muslims, as well as of those Muslims who are perceived to be too friendly with, for example, their Christian neighbours.

One obvious place to start such sowing of the seeds of hatred is in a university. We met a Christian from Botswana as well as a young man from Kenya bearing a Muslim name but of a mixed faith background. He had chosen to identify with the Christian faith of his maternal grandmother. The contrast between them could not have been greater in terms of the treatment they received from their friends. The young man from Botswana was not able to talk about his faith even to his best friend, who was a Muslim. His friend knew and tolerated the fact that he was friends with a Christian. But, as Anjum and I used to say when we worked together in Blackburn, 'Who on earth wants simply to be tolerated?' All this means is that you put up with someone. But if the image of God is in each and every single human soul then it can never be the case that people should merely be tolerated. They should be respected and honoured for their God-given humanity. In this case, it would be more accurate to say that the young man's Christian faith was really ignored by his Muslim friend. They played football together and listened to music together – music which, the Christian young man acknowledged was probably *haram*, that's the Arabic word for forbidden, for his Muslim friend. But they couldn't have that conversation either. They had, instead, to tip-toe around one another's true identity.

For the young man of a mixed faith background – bearing a Muslim name but choosing to be Christian – things, in one way, were similar. He, too, could not talk about his faith – which, as both of us observed, must have been agony for him since he was one of the most talkative and smilingly engaging people we met anywhere on our travels. But at least he suffered no suspicion from his friends because he bore a name that identified him – at least on the surface – as Muslim.

I know what you'll say to me now! Wasn't it the case that I spent quite a long time commenting on the significance of names in the last letter – even going so far as to suggest that in someone's name lies perhaps the secret of their calling? I did indeed. And you'd be right, of course, to go on to point out to me that this may not make much sense in the case of a Christian young man with a Muslim name that he received at birth. But you'll have to trust me that it does in fact make wonderful sense. The sad thing is that I can't prove it to you by telling you what his name is because to name either of these young men – and you'll see that I've been careful not to do so – would be to put them in danger. In the next letter, I shall similarly be unable to include the names of those involved. I wasn't even told them. And I shan't be able to tell you who told me the story or where it was told.

Jesus promised that he had come so that the humanity of all God's children might be freed. The humanity of each of the people and communities that I've talked about today has been compromised since they can't easily be who they are or worship in the buildings they'd wish to construct. However, their dream of being fully human has not been destroyed by their circumstances.

Lord Jesus,
you set your followers in contexts
where they are sometimes unable to be themselves:
be with them as they must worship you in secret
or hide their identity from those around them.
Help them to know that you see
what is done in the secret of the human heart
and that you judge each of us by our intention
to love you and our neighbour as we love ourselves.
With love, Daddy

Dear Chris,

Dreams can guide us, warn us and, sometimes, they can also show us the way out of difficult situations. Joseph, according to Christian Scriptures, is guided through a dream to name Jesus. We, as Muslims, do not have this narrative in our Scriptures. But we accept Jesus as a 'miracle' baby born by divine intervention.

Our journey to Zanzibar showed us how people dream of having peace. Yet at the same time people know it isn't just a dream — living together peacefully must become a reality. People from Christian and Islamic beliefs lived under one roof. Yet, something happened to shatter their dreams of peace! Someone ruined the dream! Who was it?

We witnessed the Christian female students who had to wear head-coverings for their own safety, and we met the Muslim imam whose face had been disfigured by someone throwing acid. His crime was that he spoke about integration and peace thorough dialogue. Both communities are living in fear! Both dreaming of what they once had! Both communities have their history to fall back on but, sadly, the new generation does not have the same luxury. Young people are growing up witnessing conflict and the peaceful past is only a dream for them.

What was so amazing was to see how comfortable these young people were talking about their experimentation with another faith, from Christianity to Islam, and from Islam to Christianity — but fear was not too far away! One young Muslim man retained his Muslim name but wore a cross round his neck. Some would say that this was a contradiction, but for him there was no contradiction. He is on a journey!

'And you, when will you begin that long journey into yourself?' — Rumi

Yours, Anjum

Wednesday 14 December

Dear Jonny,

A minister – again, as I explained yesterday, I can't name him or the country he was talking about – met us on our travels. I can't even tell you where. But I can tell you that he said roughly this:

'In one of the countries I visit, where Islam is very strong, I can't dress in a dog collar, I can't take with me a Bible or a cross or a prayer book. The last time I went I was asked to baptise some women and men who wanted to convert from Islam. We met on a Friday lunchtime because Christians aren't allowed to worship in public at all – certainly not on a Sunday! We met in a compound where there are a few Christians. We met in one of their homes. We couldn't sing hymns because that would attract attention from the Muslim neighbours. The catechumens (that's the name for those preparing for baptism) came forward. They'd been prepared over a number of weeks. They wanted me to give them some advice. I was frankly at a loss as to what to say. Should they be getting baptised at all, I wondered? Because to baptise in a country that does not welcome any other faith than Islam is potentially to invite people into martyrdom. Is that my job as a minister, to line people up to be killed for their faith? I seriously wondered whether they should do it. Yet, who am I to stand in the way of God's gift and grace? I thought hard. I swallowed my reservations and then I tried to set out a framework for them that might work. Each one of them continued to live in a Muslim home. I told them that they must do their *salat* (that's the five daily prayers). The men must go to mosque and pray with the other men of their families and communities. They must do this even on Fridays when their fellow Christians are meeting. All of them must live outwardly as Muslims. They must work to find a time when they could meet in secret for worship, and to encourage one another in their Christian faith. But they must not put themselves in danger to do so.'

'As I said this,' he continued, 'I wondered if I was compromising in the other direction. I was so concerned for their safety. But was I not now denying them the very pathway of discipleship that is the Christian way? I was consigning them to be individuals not members of the body of Christ. I was making them say prayers that they now did not believe. But I held firm in what I was saying. God, I concluded, knows the secrets of all hearts. He will see their intentions and reward them.'

The minister got back on his plane and returned to his community where Christianity is not only tolerated but it is respected and encouraged. He was crest-fallen. We could see it in his face. He simply did not know whether what he'd said to those new Christians was right. Had he lacked courage, he wondered? Had he failed them, failed God?

It's the sort of story after which it's pretty redundant to add very much. Perhaps prayer and silence are the only responses that we may make.

It's impossible sometimes, Lord
to know what you want.

It seems crazy that you would call
people to follow you
in places where to do so
is an open invitation
not to fullness of life
but to death.
Only you seem to know what you're doing.
Show us how to follow you wherever we are
and especially to assist everyone
in such places of danger.

With love, Daddy

Dear Chris,

A nameless country — but is it really 'Islam' that is strong? Or a version of Islam that has been upheld by those who are supported by Western governments?! Sadly, despotic leadership is needed by those who seek to exploit and rule by supporting puppet regimes. The minister did not fail the people nor did he fail God, because God sees one's intentions. As a Muslim, I believe that our actions are dependent on our intentions and our intentions are in our hearts. God can see within our hearts — so, he knows our intentions!

'Actions are judged by one's intentions.' — Prophet Muhammad (pbuh)

Yours, Anjum

Thursday 15 December

*D*ear Jonny,

I wish somehow that I could write something more cheerful at this point in Advent. But the trouble with waiting in hope, which is what we're meant to be doing, is that the hope for which we wait so longingly is too often confused with optimism. There's too much that's so utterly terrifying about the world right now to be optimistic that things will get better. But I am hopeful. Perhaps, now is the moment to say why. But to get to the reason we have again, I'm afraid, to delve into the misery of life.

Undoubtedly, one of the more difficult aspects of the time that Anjum and I spent in Lahore involved meetings with people about what's called the 'blasphemy law'. It was the British who first introduced some sort of blasphemy law in the land that eventually became Pakistan. To some, a blasphemy law is there to prevent insult being given to faith communities. So it would prevent people, for instance, saying insulting things about Jesus or Mohammad. To others, it limits free speech since those holding this view would argue that it means certain topics can't be debated openly and remain off limits.

My purpose is not to debate the rights and the wrongs of such a law. What is most significant in Pakistan is the way in which the original blasphemy law has been extended, not only to cover many different categories of possible offence, but also to place the burden of proof on the accused rather than the accuser. In a normal case, you are innocent until proven guilty. To most people that is one of the most important things about any legal system. But in terms of the blasphemy law in Pakistan, this is reversed. The accused is thus guilty until proven innocent.

Anjum and I had long conversations with two very courageous lawyers. One is a man called Naeem Shakir, an attorney of the Supreme Court and defending counsel in a very high profile blasphemy case: that of a woman called Asia Bibi. The other is a woman called Asma Jahangir, senior advocate of the Supreme Court, former chairperson of Pakistan's Human Rights Commission, and a woman who was imprisoned in the 1980s for her participation in the movement to restore democracy during military rule in Pakistan. We had a long lunch with both of them and each changed the venue for the lunch several times because they knew that they were being followed. The third person with whom we had lunch was equally remarkable, a man called Joseph Francis to whom Her Majesty The Queen has awarded an MBE – as she has to Anjum. Joseph has done some important work through the Centre for Legal Aid Assistance and Settlement (CASS) in order to address many of the blasphemy cases.

Sometimes it's supposed that the blasphemy law is used against minorities. This is certainly not the case. Terrifyingly, anyone may bring a blasphemy case against another person and once the case has been brought the accused will most likely be detained indefinitely. This is a horrifyingly unjust situation. But it also suits the Pakistan Government that the law is framed in this way because it creates fear and insecurity among the whole population. As I write, there are around five hundred cases being tried under the blasphemy law that involve Muslim Pakistanis

This is proof of the way in which the law is actually used as a means for the state to terrorise its own citizens and to create an atmosphere where people are afraid to speak out both publicly and privately.

The morning Anjum and I spent interviewing the families of some of the victims of this appalling law is one that I will never forget. It was difficult for me since they were speaking in Urdu, which meant that what was said had to be translated by Anjum, who grew up in Karachi. This made things much slower for the family as we spoke and, I feared, more upsetting. But it was also emotionally difficult because the first group of people to whom we were speaking were a father, whose wife had been imprisoned because she was accused of blasphemy, and their children, Yasir aged 17, Zeeshan 14, Muhsan 8, Sadia 5 and Hassan 3. The 8 year old Muhsan was sat next to me crying pitifully throughout the time we spent with them. I was trying to hold his hand in a vain attempt to comfort him. But he was pretty much inconsolable. It turned out that he felt totally responsible for what had happened to his mother, Shamshad Bibi.

After we had spoken to Muhammed Ahmed, her husband, we were given an English summary of the case to read but this varied somewhat from what Muhammed struggled to tell us in very broken sentences, so I'm going to try to put both versions together and make the best sense of them I can for you.

It seems that Shamshad, who was 32 at the time we spoke to Muhammed, was accused of insulting the Holy Qu'ran. Suffering from what are called mental health issues when the events unfolded, she was in the habit of going to the local mosque as a way of deriving comfort. Either she herself dropped a copy of the Qu'ran in unclean water, in drainage, on the way to the mosque early one morning, or Muhsan, now 8, did so returning from *Madrassa* (which is, basically, a place where children learn

about their religion) one evening. Based on Muhsan's near hysteria
as he told me this story this seemed entirely possible. Whatever
actually happened, an imam filed a complaint against Shamshad
at the local police station. He did so, surely knowing full well,
that for dropping the Qu'ran all she had to do was to make
amends by paying a small sum of money to charity and offering
some prayers.

Instead, Shamshad and her oldest child Yasir were arrested
on the same day and detained for eight days. At this point Yasir
was freed. Mohammed begged the imam to understand the state
of her mind and the fact that she simply couldn't think things
through, as well as the fact that she simply would never have
intended to drop the Qu'ran in a puddle of dirty water, let alone
defame the name of the prophet as had been suggested. He did
so in the hope that the imam would withdraw the case. But he
didn't. Mohammed then had to take his children to another village
because those associated with a person accused of blasphemy
can face name-calling, physical violence and even death threats.

Shamshad received no treatment in jail as her mental health
deteriorated. She was repeatedly made to attend hearings in court
unsupported. Mohammed's pleas about this were completely
ignored. He lacked money to pay for the lawyer's fees, hence
he turned to Joseph Francis and CASS for help. Shamshad has
already been in prison for three years, which is almost the whole
of Hassan's life. He too was inconsolable and held my other hand
throughout the interview.

Where, you may wonder, is the hope in this story, which I
have tried to tell dispassionately, not because I didn't feel anger
at the injustice of it and not because I wasn't crying myself, but
because when told without much emotion the idiocy of it all
becomes all the more clear. The hope surely lies not just in the
amazing resilience and courage of Shamshad, Mohammed and

their family (in fact, Shamshad became so ill in prison that most people expected she would have died long ago). But the hope must also surely lie in the fact that people like Naeem, Asma and Joseph are prepared to use all the energy they have – at great risk to their own personal safety – to fight for justice. Here surely are three lights in the darkness of Advent, three roses blossoming towards the summer in winter, which is how Robert Herrick refers to Christmas in one of his poems.

Lord Jesus,

when all is dark

when hope has

all but been extinguished

you send light and summer

to restore the vision of your kingdom:

turn us always to look

at the roses that bloom above the thorns

and make us beacons of light for one another.

With love, Daddy

Dear Chris

Pakistan, the country where I was born. Yet, in Lahore my family and I are still considered as 'refugees / Muhajirs.' My parents came from India to settle in a country that would be a place where all were treated with respect, regardless of one's colour, creed or faith. If this was the vision of that time, sadly, this is not the reality that we witnessed in Lahore.

How can a country that was conceived to be a place for those who believe in One God treat its minorities so unsympathetically? The blasphemy law of Pakistan has become a thorn in the side of human rights! Eighty percent of those who are impacted by this law are Muslims. Many who have spoken up against it have paid a heavy price with their lives. Salman Taseer, Governor of Pakistan was murdered by his own guard. His crime: to ask for Asia Bibi (a Christian woman on death row) to be released! Shabaz Bhatti, Federal Minister for Minorities, is another example. He was a man with whom I shared a platform just a few months before he was murdered in Lahore. I was once told that 'a country's character is judged according to its treatment of its minorities.' I wonder what the founding fathers of this country would say . . . I know my own parents, who lost much when they left India, feel the pain deeply.

But it is better to light a candle than to curse the darkness. And, human rights activists, lawyers and women's groups are lighting a candle for those who cannot speak up. It is so important that we do not forget those who are striving for justice in Pakistan! Neither should we forget those who are languishing in jail for their faith!

'With faith, discipline and selfless devotion to duty, there is nothing worthwhile that you cannot achieve.' — Muhammad Ali Jinnah (Father of Pakistan)

Yours, Anjum

Friday 16 December

Dear Jonny,

An outbreak of angels above the fields over Bethlehem heralds the birth of Jesus. In Luke's version (chapter 2 verses 1 to 20) the glory of the Lord shines all around the shepherds. The word for glory, *doxa*, is one of the most important words in the Bible. When God's glory is experienced it means that God is there – as on the mountain when Moses collects the Ten Commandments, or later on the mountain of what's called the Transfiguration, when Jesus is revealed to Peter, James and John as the Son of God. As Matthew reminded us, one of Jesus' names is Emmanuel – God is, indeed, with us!

There is a lot of symbolism here. Zechariah's song – which the church commonly refers to as the *Benedictus* – promises that the day-spring from on high will dawn on God's people. The shepherds are representatives of the whole of Israel. Luke has connected the event to the whole empire. It's of worldwide significance by his references to the census. You've experienced one of these in your life. But you probably don't remember it as the last census in the UK happened in 2011, when you were just four years old. It's when the government – in Luke's story the Roman authorities – collect information about all citizens: who is living where, what their employment is, what religion they follow, if any, and so on. This is why the heavily pregnant Mary travels with Joseph to the town which is central for his tribe. He's descended from King David so they go from Galilee to Bethlehem. It's also why there's no room for them to stay. You'll remember all that from several nativity plays with which you've been involved and from countless Christmas services.

The Good News has to be heard first somewhere. The shepherds are poor folk. They are outsiders economically. They don't have much in the way of material resources. But they are insiders in terms of faith: they are members of the Jewish community. It's appropriate that they of all people should meet the shepherd of the flock of Israel. Later we will meet a group of Magi – astrologers – who are insiders where wealth is concerned but outsiders to the faith of Jesus. Luke has already introduced us to this idea. Everyone belongs in the Kingdom of God that has broken into the world through Jesus.

> God of glory,
> you show yourself to the poor in spirit
> because you know their desire
> for the richness of your love.
> You show yourself to the pure in heart
> because it is purity of living that you require.
> You show yourself to those who hunger
> and thirst for righteousness
> because you know this is why
> they come to your manger throne:
> help all who follow the road to Bethlehem
> to know you as the source of perfect blessing
> and peace.

With love, Daddy

Dear Chris,

Bethlehem, a town you and I have visited on several occasions with great difficulty due to the wall and its hindrance to visitors. What a day it must have been when Jesus was born? Mary / Mariam, a young girl, giving birth to a son who will challenge the establishment of the day, shake the foundations of its leadership and become one of the greatest prophets of the day — from my Islamic perspective of course!

Songs and hymns celebrating Jesus' birth have reminded us of this eventful day. But of course the actual day of his birth is disputed, not only by the Christians themselves but also in my own religious community! Does it matter when he was born? The fact that he was born as a guide for his people is sufficient. The good news about his birth filtered to the Jewish community of his day. It had to, Jesus was Jewish. But did his birth become a threat to the Jewish leadership…?

'We should live our lives as though Christ was coming this afternoon.' — Jimmy Carter

Yours, Anjum

Saturday 17 December

Dear Jonny,

In Advent 2014 I found myself in Dubai. Some of our friends wondered whether I'd suddenly come into some money and was going there to shop! As you know, I absolutely hate shopping of all kinds, except when the shelves are lined with books! So what was I doing in a nice hotel in one of the world's richest places?

For those of us who are members of the International Advisory Group for USPG – which really gave birth to these letters by inviting Anjum and me to undertake the workshops, interviews and seminars that lie behind them – it was actually the most central place for us to meet. So we came from Tonga, the United Kingdom, Sri Lanka, Mozambique, Cyprus and Tanzania to help plan the future of what's done on the ground in many countries across the Anglican Communion. We worked hard during the day, from dawn until dusk. But at night time we had some visits to see what the Anglican Church in the United Arab Emirates (UAE), within which Dubai is situated, is doing.

I should mention first that UAE is, of course, a majority Muslim country. The hotel was nonetheless full of Christmas trees and decorations. We worshipped with the local Anglican chaplaincy which hosts both Friday and Sunday services. In a Muslim country some are required to work on Sundays, so they must go to church on Fridays when the Muslims are at mosque. We were there for Friday worship and as we emerged from the Eucharist I was struck by an enormous poster advertising 'Carols in the Desert' that evening. You may think that Cape Town was hot when we spent Christmas there, but let me tell you it has nothing on Dubai!

One of the themes we had discussed in our meetings was the issue of migrancy. It's cropped up in these letters already a few times because it's one of the biggest realities in the life of the world. People have always moved around. Indeed, the whole of the planet was populated by a migration northwards that began in Africa. But, now, the sheer numbers of people moving for work, or for educational reasons, or to flee from conflict – for a combination of reasons to seek 'a better life' – is making migration one of the most contentious issues of our times.

There are millions of migrant workers in Dubai. Many come from the Indian subcontinent and the Philippines with the promise that the money they earn will be at such a high rate that they will be able to provide opportunities for their families back home. Most of them, interestingly, are Christians – which means that the Anglican Church in Dubai has a particular ministry to migrants. They may not all be Anglican Christians – indeed many may be Roman Catholics – but it seems that the Anglicans are seen as a focus for Christians of many denominations.

Dubai contains the tallest building in the world. It's called the Burj Khalifa. We didn't go to its top. We didn't enter it at all in fact. But we did stand beneath it.

I visited the twin towers in New York once – you'll remember me telling you how planes smashed into them in a terrorist attack on 11 September 2001, which some people now refer to as '9/11'.

I did go right to the top of one of the towers. I hate heights. I have no idea why I did it. It was simply there, I suppose, and I thought I'd just better go to the top! It was so high I can't describe to you what it felt like looking down. It was enough just to stand underneath the Burj Khalifa. But a few streets away from this building which represents wealth and status at one extreme, our drivers dropped us at hostels containing some of the workers who build the many skyscrapers of Dubai. The contrast could not have been greater.

You'll remember me telling you that I once taught at a boarding school in Cambridge. When I arrived at the school I was shocked to see the number of pupils crammed into bunk beds in small rooms. Over the five years I was there I set about working with my colleagues to transform the space by ensuring that no one ever slept in a bunk bed and by building what are called mezzanine floors to create more space.

The moment I walked into the migrant hostel for the men whom I was visiting (for reasons of privacy the men in our group visited a men's hostel and the women a women's hostel) that memory of the boarding school flashed into my head. Only here, in Dubai, the soaring heat and the lack of air conditioning made it one hundred times worse. The rooms for living and sleeping were located around a filthy common courtyard for cooking and washing clothes. Each room was about the size of, let's say, the bedroom that your mum and I share – pretty average in other words. Yet, it contained between sixteen and twenty men in bunks stacked three high. The smell, inevitably, of so many adult male bodies was terrible. But I was less embarrassed by this than by the fact that here we were a group of outsiders invading the personal space of adult men, almost all of whom were husbands and fathers. It felt wrong, somehow, to be behaving like tourists, looking at them as if they were exhibits.

Each of us did our best to overcome this shared feeling by chatting to the men. I don't know why, but for me this was one of the most tearful experiences of all the travels I've been describing. I've seen a lot worse. I stayed in Kibera and the stench of the slum was appalling, the gunshots at night frightening and the dog barking relentless. But here in this place, out of the front door of which we could see the Burj Khalifa and all that it represents of status, power and the supposed glory of human achievement, I felt like I was on the underbelly of history. Surely I was in a place where the image of God I saw in each of the faces I encountered was steadily and even systematically being erased. To be honest, I don't think the bosses who put men in these hostels can see them as human at all.

But our visit did something for them. First, it gave them a chance to tell their stories. Second, it gave them a sense of a world beyond the construction sites on which they work and the hovel in which they attempt to sleep. Third, it reminded them that they are loved.

A few years ago on a visit to Harare in Zimbabwe, I got myself into all sorts of difficulty when I took some photos outside the Anglican cathedral there. It happens to be next to the parliament and apparently photos are not, therefore, allowed for security reasons. I found this out when seven soldiers, all shouting at me, pointed their machine guns in my face and asked to see the pictures. Luckily, my camera also had a photo of you and your brothers. The men were young soldiers, doubtless either with small children themselves or with younger siblings. 'Who are they?' one of the solders asked. I explained that they were my sons. 'Cute!' said another soldier as they all passed round the camera looking at the photo and laughing. From being representatives of a government that was only too keen to shout at people, point guns in their faces and give them a torrid time they suddenly became human beings again. In fact, I had to remind them that I could see their commanding officer and that though he wasn't probably expecting them to arrest me, he was wanting them to make sure that I knew who was in charge. I actually had to say to them, 'Shout at me, otherwise you will be in trouble!' This is what they had to do as they sent me on my way.

That moment has stayed with me because it taught me not that you were cute – I knew that already though it's a phrase you would hate me to use! – but that once you connect with people on a human level things are different.

Who doesn't like small children? I know some adults seem not to be so keen. But basically pretty much everyone likes to see other people's children.

This is how I made a connection with some of those men in the hostel. They had terrible stories to tell of the money they'd been promised and of finding that actually some of their salary was deducted to pay for the awful hostel in which they lived. They had stories about the lack of health and safety on the construction sites, of the death of men – the sort of stories we have heard told in relation to the construction of football stadia in Qatar for the World Cup. But when I got out my iPhone and showed them pictures of you and your two brothers, they got out their phones and showed me their families.

I'm writing this as I sit at my desk looking into Westcott House where I've just moved to be principal. You've made a sacrifice in allowing me to take this job because you and your brothers and mummy are staying in London for a year so that your middle brother can finish his GCSE course. I know you tease me that it's my iPad, Minecraft and Clash of Clans that you miss more than me, but as we begin to experience the weekdays apart and only weekends together I do know how difficult it is for you and how much you miss me. I miss you too, all of you, more than I can say. And now I'm crying! But this arrangement is temporary.

Imagine how awful it is for the families of the migrant workers in Dubai. They are often away for two or three years at a stretch before they return home. Many of them are not highly skilled workers. They aren't probably people who've had the chance to receive much education. One of the things the Anglican priest who is their chaplain does for them is to show them how to Skype home. Some of them didn't know how to do this. Whilst I was there I watched him show a new worker how to do so, and then we were all crying as we saw his excitement at seeing his baby daughter for the very first time. But he should have actually been there. He shouldn't have had to experience this through a mobile phone. God didn't send a message to us human beings. He'd tried that before and it didn't work. No – he came in person!

> Lord God,
> face to face
> is your way of doing things.
> In a world where families
> are forced to live apart
> support all who are away
> from their loved ones:
> wipe away their tears
> and sustain them
> in the hope your coming brings.

With love, Daddy

Dear Chris,

    Christmas in Dubai with a $17 million Christmas tree and its 22 caret gold decorations somehow is not the kind of Christmas that I am used to. But each to their own! What has migration taught us all? Or what has it done for us today, when people are moving about because of political and economic situations in their own countries? The overseas workers in UAE tend to come mainly from the subcontinent for economic reasons and, very sadly, their treatment leaves much to be desired. The living conditions of the migrant workers are appalling and disgraceful. These poor people leave their families for long periods only to be treated like animals! How can their 'masters' be so inhuman? Where is humanity in all this? Pity that these people do not understand the actions of their own Prophet Muhammad whose household was such that no servant was ever abused physically or verbally.

    People travel for all sorts of reasons, persecution or poverty. I like to think that migration of Muslims in a country like ours has assisted 'faith' to be visible in the public square. Our own country seems to be more secular than when I was a little girl. You know, Sunday was the Sabbath and shops were closed, carol singers were a must for Christmas (I actually went carol singing with my Christian friends), and the story of the birth of Jesus was told by many — not only in Churches, but also in our media. Sadly, secularization of religion has pushed Christianity much more into the private domain. Muslim migrants tend to be a little more practicing in their faith and the external manifestation of their faith is very visible. Headscarves, beards and hats in the public space are very difficult to ignore. Isn't this a good thing though? Or is it really the case, as some would have us believe, 'Watch out! The Muslims are coming!' To be honest, I thought we were already here!

    Having religion in the public square is so very important because it is in the public space that we get to see each other's humanity. As soon as we interact at a human level we cross over many difficult bridges!

    'A believer wishes for others what he wishes for himself.' — Prophet Muhammad

Yours, Anjum

Sunday 18 December

*D*ear Jonny,

Face to face contact, you'll recall, is God's preferred means of engaging with the world. That's why Anjum and I actually visited the countries whose stories lie behind this journey through Advent to Christmas. We couldn't get under the skin of what some Sri Lankans or South Africans are feeling, we couldn't do it through Skype. We had to go there ourselves and be guided by those who live and work in the contexts we visited. I can only hope that they would recognise their words, stories and experiences in what I've written.

Why am I emphasising this point now?

Because we are close to the birth of Jesus, the one who knew that the only answer was literally to get under our skin and to come to visit us as God become a human being. But also because Christians can easily forget that the way God works is meant to be an example to follow. Christians in our part of the world can still too often fall back into thinking that they must go and sort everyone else out, ignoring what we call the complexities of context and culture which change the way in which things work in all sorts of subtle ways.

When I first went to Cape Town as an ordinand from Westcott House I was always wondering why every meeting started late until someone said to me, 'Look, Chris, you have the watch but we have the time!' It was a good lesson and actually I've never worn a watch since. I now just irritate other people by asking them the time! But the point I'm making is about the way things look different in different places.

Usually on our visits, I've been asked to lead Bible studies with groups of clergy or lay people – and on one occasion we did this across a group of Christians and Muslims. I love the Bible, as I hope you can tell. I love the fact that when you listen to its stories you can always find ways in which they connect with life now.

But I find the challenge of leading Bible studies in different countries and contexts a heavy one. Since the interpretation that I bring of the Bible – in other words, the way in which I understand its meaning or the lens through which I see it – is conditioned by the fact that I am a middle-aged (that's the first time I've ever admitted that in writing!) British male who is mostly pink. So the way I see things is conditioned by all these and many other factors. I haven't read books on the Bible in Korean or Swahili for instance, or Chinese or Afrikaans. I've read a few in German and French, but most books on the Bible that I've read have been in English.

So when I'm in a particular country I do try to lead the Bible workshops in such a way that those who are participants are not merely passive learners but teachers too.

In Sri Lanka, for instance, I was actually asked to lead a Bible study on the next text to which we need to turn in our journey through Luke and Matthew. This is the story in which you once played a part in a nativity play at John Keble Church when you proudly walked in as one of the Magi. So I'm going to show you in this and the next couple of letters how I worked with the priests of the Diocese of Colombo.

First of all, I tried to give them some background. We read the story (Matthew 2:1-12) and I offered some reflections on it based on what a priest who taught me as a child, David Isitt, used to call Close Attention to the Text (CAT).

I haven't so far printed the text of the Bible readings at which we've looked. I've usually told them to you in my own words. But as I began my first session in Colombo by using the New Revised Standard Version of the Bible, here is the text we were reading.

> In the time of King Herod, after Jesus was born in Bethlehem of Judea, wise men from the East came to Jerusalem, asking, 'Where is the child who has been born king of the Jews? For we observed his star at its rising, and have come to pay him homage.' When King Herod heard this, he was frightened, and all Jerusalem with him; and calling together all the chief priests and scribes of the people, he inquired of them where the Messiah was to be born. They told him, 'In Bethlehem of Judea; for so it has been written by the prophet:
>
> 'And you, Bethlehem, in the land of Judah,
> are by no means least among the rulers of Judah;
> for from you shall come a ruler
> who is to shepherd my people Israel.'

Then Herod secretly called for the wise men and learned from them the exact time when the star had appeared. Then he sent them to Bethlehem, saying, 'Go and search diligently for the child; and when you have found him, bring me word so that I may also go and pay him homage.' When they had heard the king, they set out; and there, ahead of them, went the star that they had seen at its rising, until it stopped over the place where the child was. When they saw that the star had stopped, they were overwhelmed with joy. On entering the house, they saw the child with Mary his mother; and they knelt down and paid him homage. Then, opening their treasure chests, they offered him gifts of gold, frankincense, and myrrh. And having been warned in a dream not to return to Herod, they left for their own country by another road.

Before we get into what this very familiar story might mean, I'd like you to think about it for yourself today and tonight when you sleep, because what you hear in it is as important, if not more so, than what I will say about it.

Holy God,
the stories of your love
have gone out into every land.
They feel different
wherever they are heard.
New insights come to the surface
in every community:
give us the imagination
to cherish these,
to see your word and your truth
not as letters on a piece of paper
or laws in a book
but as a diamond shining
from every possible angle.

With love, Daddy

Dear Chris,

Face to face conversations can never be replaced by Skype, telephone or emails. We could not have gathered such extraordinary snippets of news and stories without actually going over to the places that we visited. I understand that Christians believe God transformed himself and became human so that people could relate and understand his teaching. That he came face to face with humanity!

I appreciate face to face conversations and take the lead from my own Prophet who says that one needs to have guidance from a teacher who can come face to face to help get over difficult situations and understand the other. I guess that is why many people have difficulty with the veil in our society, which hides the face of the other!

Different situations demand different strategies. But somehow I will never be able to get used to doing things at either the 11th hour or with a laid back attitude about time. I guess I am a control freak — it's my conditioning! I will never forget when once I was in India and we were supposed to arrive at a school at 10.00 am. The car broke down and we were stranded for over an hour. My thoughts were with the school kids who would be waiting for us, how disappointing for them! I could not believe that when we arrived hours later they were still there sitting on their little chairs without any air conditioning or fans, waiting for these 'important' people from the UK. I have never felt so hopelessly embarrassed! I learned that I was judging the audience according to my own experiences in my own country, where no school would have made their children wait for three hours. But in India it was the done thing!

Recognising our audience helps us to deliver information. However, more importantly, it helps us to interact with those who come from different cultural / religious backgrounds.

As Herod was scheming and planning to harm baby Jesus, God guided the three wise men through a dream and they avoided being part of a terrible plan. We seek guidance from Jesus through his message. He may not be present in physical form with us, but his message lives on for all those who can understand.

> ...and Jesus said, 'Indeed God is my Lord and your Lord and worship Him, that is the straight path.' – Qur'an 19:36

Yours, Anjum

Monday 19 December

Dear Jonny,

Every text has many contexts. One of them is, as I suggested yesterday, the lens through which you see and hear and feel the story. I don't know what you've thought about since yesterday. I shall look forward to hearing how you experience the story for yourself. But I want to try and say something first about the way people in Matthew's context might have seen, heard and felt things.

While Luke's Gospel is largely written for Gentiles (that is, non-Jews) and gently introduces them to things Jewish, the Gospel of Matthew is largely written for an audience with a Jewish background.

Quite how shockingly good news the Gospel was in Matthew's day is hard for us to take in of course. We've all been to so many presentations of the nativity that we can't perhaps get beyond Melchior, Caspar and Balthasar, the three names given to the Magi by the English theologian the Venerable Bede. A theologian, by the way, is someone who thinks about God and the world, and who also speaks or writes about it. Bede lived in the eighth century and built on an earlier idea that there must have been

three wise men because there were three gifts. We simply don't
know if this was the case.

We've noticed that Matthew's genealogy really does deserve
careful study. Find out the stories of the swindlers, cheats and
liars within it and you really do get a sense of how shocking it
would have been for Matthew's hearers, and later readers, to learn
that they were part of Jesus' family tree. We can also tell the
sort of people Matthew was addressing based on the contents
of this genealogy. It suggests to us that Matthew is up against
some Jewish-Christians rather too sure of themselves in terms
of their Jewish heritage. Matthew slaps them round the face with
the reality of the cheats and low-life characters who form the
physical lineage of Jesus. 'Don't be so sure of yourselves and your
tradition,' he's saying. The wine skins are being burst.'

And so to chapter two and the story of the Magi. We
cannot imagine the shock to those first hearers on the Sunday
that Matthew's Gospel was first proclaimed. First the low-life
lot then the sorcerers. The Greek word is *magoi*, Magi. We don't
know whether they were wise or even whether they were men!
Mummy reminds me that had they been women they wouldn't of
course have left such ridiculous gifts for a baby. They'd have been
much more practical! But before I get into trouble with mummy's
stereotypes – which in this case means saying that people act in
a particular way because they are male or female – or add any
of my own, let's just be sure that these Magi were actually low-
life characters. That's not what we've usually come to believe.
We think of them as rather grand, as kings. Yet, check out the
references to *magos* in the New Testament.

In chapter 8 of the Acts of the Apostles we learn of a man
called Simon, a successful *magos* who then tries to use his skills
as a sorcerer when he becomes a Christian. He probably sees the
chance to make some money with a new audience. Peter rejects

this possibility very firmly and it seems to have affected the way Christians see sorcery ever since. Another sorcerer called Elymas from a place called Paphos in Cyprus appears later in the Acts of the Apostles chapter 13, when he tries his skills as a sort of mediator – perhaps better to say medium – between Paul and Sergius Paulus, who is the local governor. But Paul is not impressed. He calls Elymas the son of a devil and an enemy of justice.

So, against what we've been led to believe, the Magi don't have much standing. They may be the most impressive characters to be in a nativity play – I don't think you fought in the wings with other children as to who would carry the most glittering gift but I've seen nativity plays where that's happened! But in the days of Herod – that narrows things down to the period between 37 and 4BC – they were seen as political schemers. They were the folk you called on to read the stars in order to work out what was going on politically, to see who was up to what. They were pawns of the powerful. They most often said simply what people wanted to hear.

Before we run away with criticism of the Magi and their fake profession, we do have to admit that in this case they did actually get it right. Despite all the trickery and deceit they might have been used to, they turn up with the right question and having made a long journey. Incidentally, we know how long it must have been. This is because when Herod decides to slay all the infants under two, he's recognising that the star appeared two years before. So that's the time from which the threat dates. Clearly this journey was no quick trot to Jerusalem. This was an arduous, purposeful quest for truth.

Of course the insiders – the chief priests and the scribes – see the question itself as a threat. These insiders seem to see truth itself as inherently threatening.

Only Gentiles would refer to Jesus as 'king of the Jews'. Jewish people, as in verse 4, would refer to Jesus as Messiah. The very mention of all this causes Herod to take fright – and the word that's used for fright in verse 3 is the one that's used when the disciples see Jesus walking on water towards them and they're too afraid to follow suit. So this word for frightened or fearful is one that's used when you talk about people who haven't got enough belief. Herod cannot believe in a Messiah – he sees a Messiah as a threat to his own power. But the sorcerers and their apprentices believe.

There's a really important point that Matthew is making here and this is to make us realise that God's truth is so often entrusted to the so-called outsiders.

I appointed Anjum to the staff of Blackburn Cathedral – and it was the first time in the world that a Muslim had been appointed to the staff of a cathedral – to try and bring the communities of northern England closer together. I lost count of the times when she was the one who said – 'You Christians, you used to fast. We got our Ramadan from you. What happened to your Lent? Now you give up things but you don't really fast.' That's just one example of how the supposed outsider so often proves to be the custodian of so-called insider information. 'The truth must dazzle gradually,' as the poet Emily Dickinson has it, 'or everyone be blind.'

As a result of this insight about truth given to the supposed outsider, we must ask ourselves whether we stop or block the truth because of our own egos and selfish concerns. Do we prevent Epiphany (that's the word used to describe the fact that Jesus is 'shown' to the whole world in this story and not just to the Jewish shepherds who came to see him from the hills outside Bethlehem)? Other questions are also prompted. Do we play Herod's role too often? Do we become so excited with power and influence that we forget the truth that power is shown in weakness? Do we scheme like Herod, call people secretly together, make ourselves so much a part of the culture of scheming that, let's face it, can too often be church life as we know it? My goodness, even at your age you have pointed out to me some of the silly games that church people play!

'Go and search diligently,' Herod says. But he's not after truth, he's after self-interest. He's protecting his territory. Do we behave in the same way?

These are scary questions. I'm inserting them now because when you're older you'll notice the way in which people tend to avoid them. As the poet TS Eliot once said, people 'cannot bear very much reality.' You may even be tempted to avoid it yourself. But we ought not to avoid it as I suspect too often we do.

I'm powerfully aware of the fact that I've just stopped being a parish priest. So I'm asking myself each of the questions I've listed and I'm not always pleased with the way they convict me in my weakness, my inadequacy, my hopeless grasping after the illusions of authority and power – both of which are far too easy to abuse. I'm also bringing them into the open (because that's what Epiphany does) since the point of Matthew's narrative is to include all in what we call the revelation of Christ. Matthew wants to assert that this King, this God of the gutter, is for everyone. His coming ought to be the death of sorcery because star-gazing isn't needed in his light. And, yet, so often we read the negative characters in such stories as other people, not ourselves. We are the goodies. We clutch our gifts and rush off to Bethlehem to do homage, to kneel and worship. But not always before we've got ourselves thoroughly immersed in the murkier world of Jerusalem with its double-standards and religious game-playing.

Yet these magi were wise indeed. They saw the game-playing heart of the religious establishment for what it was and they departed another way. Thank God for the folk in our communities – Anjum and I have met them throughout our visits – who are brave enough to say, 'No, don't do it that way, try this one!' My goodness, those of us in sacred positions of leadership and trust need the creativity of such people to rescue us from ourselves!

> God of surprises,
> you use some pretty strange people
> to get your message across
> and to reveal your truth.
> After all, you used the sorcerers
> and their apprentices
> to show that the star
> from on high
> shines on everyone.
> Help me never to prevent anyone
> from knowing this truth:
> make me a channel
> of peace through which
> your light shines.

With love, Daddy

Dear Chris,

So were the magoi kings, as I remember from the hymn 'we three kings from orient are…'? If so, does it mean that they were also wise? I remember reading the story about those people called magoi, whose leader was prophet Daniel. Twenty two years ago I was searching for a name for my unborn baby. I knew I was going to have a baby boy and I wanted a name from either the Qur'an or the Hadiths. Prophet Daniel is not mentioned in the Qur'an but his name, appears in some Hadiths. I came across prophet Daniel's name and knew instantly that that was the name I would want to call my son.

The Magi came with gifts of gold, frankincense and myrrh. These gifts were not of poor people but were the things given by the rich. So might they have been kings and magicians? Only God knows! My understanding of the Magi is that they used to interpret dreams and visions and they were well respected in their locality. They were obviously wise because they realised that Herod was using them to meet his own agenda. So I guess political leadership has always abused people of faith! Instead of sharing the Good News political leadership hides the truth. Thank goodness for those who can turn away from wickedness and show us the correct path to follow.

'Guide us to the straight path.' – Qur'an 1:6

Yours, Anjum

Tuesday 20 December

Dear Jonny,

It's taken me much longer than I thought it would to give you some idea of what happens when we gather together to read the Bible in workshops all over the world. Perhaps I should have done that at the start of these letters rather than when we are so close to Christmas… But I hope that you can see how exciting they are. Anglicans are often terribly afraid of the Bible, and we don't get much beyond hearing it preached upon or occasionally reading the odd passage here or there. But it's really the most amazing book. There's so much to discover, and as I've said a few times, different contexts produce different angles.

When I was a music student about thirty years ago I used to go to more lectures given by theologians than by musicians. I tended to find them more interesting! One of these was given by a delightful, smiling, Sri Lankan, Fr Aloysius Pieris. He was short in stature but huge in wisdom. I can honestly say that of the thousands of lectures and sermons I have heard in my life I can remember very few. I'm sure when you're older you'll be saying that about mine too! But I remember very clearly Fr Aloysius' interpretation of the Magi. It blew me away, as they say, and a few years later when I began to study theology I learned that he was one of the most widely respected Liberation Theologians in the world. His interpretation was actually contained in his first and most widely read book, *An Asian Theology of Liberation*.

Liberation Theologians are a group who really take the context within which the Bible is read very seriously. They argue – they must surely be right in this – that the Gospel is designed to set people free; therefore, the job of every disciple, each follower of Jesus, is to play a part in setting free the people with whom they live and work.

Sri Lanka is a complex place in this regard. It's only recently emerged from a terrible civil war. The fighting has stopped but there is much freedom for people to gain.

When I knew I'd be going to Colombo with Anjum I specifically asked if we could meet Fr Aloysius, who lives on the edge of the city, and who has spent much of his life building relationships with the predominant Buddhist culture and religious framework of Sri Lanka. I intended to take my copy of the book in which he talks about the Magi. But I forgot! I didn't see this as a problem, though. I thought at least one of the priests in the workshop would no doubt know Fr Aloysius' interpretation, given how well respected he is by people of every faith in Sri Lanka.

You can imagine my slight surprise when I discovered that the clergy were not confident in sketching Fr Aloysius' interpretation. So, ironically, the pink outsider – that's me – had to have a go. But we all agreed that as this was a story about the impact of the outsiders, perhaps what happened was appropriate! I'll just repeat roughly what I said. For Fr Aloysius's Sri Lankan interpretation went something as follows.

Fr. Aloysius saw the whole of Matthew chapter 2 verses 1 to 12 as a threefold drama: search, disillusionment and discovery.

The first act, the search, took its cue from the star seen in the east drawing the magi into the journey to do homage to the newborn king. Light appeared in the east not the west. The west didn't know the truth, though it supposed it did. But truth was not found at the supposed centre of power, in Jerusalem. It was found on what the centre saw as the margins. Christ was revealed in the east before the west. You can tell why for a pink Englishman this was exciting, revolutionary stuff, when I first heard it! The star invites the Magi onto an arduous journey. I seem to remember Fr Aloysius writing that orientalists don't know short cuts! They saw the light and wanted to find its source. It led them westward and it took a long time to get there.

The second act, the disillusionment. These serious eastern folk then meet complacent western ones (complacent means that they think they know it all and have nothing more to learn, when this actually isn't the case). The west is in darkness, but the east is following the light. The west hasn't even noticed the star. It hasn't even noticed its own darkness. The west actually first hears the Good News from the eastern sages who want to know where truth is – not who he is. They want to experience truth for themselves. Herod is frightened. In his unbelieving fear none of this sounds like good tidings to him. He doesn't feel the joy that these Magi feel and the Greek words for their joy will later be used by the women at the empty tomb (Matthew 28:8) as they too feel the same joy. Herod will stop at nothing to help his fears to go away. If a holocaust of babies is what it takes, so be it. So the eastern sages find the holy city not to be a place of welcome, truth or enlightenment. It's not where the word of God is.

The third act, the discovery. A labourer's hut is where the centre of the universe is situated. The Christ whom Asia seeks is found on the knees of a peasant woman who is a carpenter's wife. This is the end of the quest. Asian wisdom sees them rightly bypass the west. It's not needed for Christ to be proclaimed in Asia.

When I first heard Fr Aloysius' interpretation, his contextual reading offered me a powerful corrective to the sort of Western dominated interpretation to which we're used. And, I think this interpretation still challenges us today.

I went on to say to the priests in Colombo that I thought such an understanding (we sometimes call it a reading) of the story surely empowers each of us with the knowledge that the light dawning in Asia and the showing forth of God in Christ in Sri Lanka is good news for people like you and me in Britain. Indeed, it is Good News for all people! We have, as we've often found in these journeys, so much to learn from one another.

> Teach us, Lord Jesus
> that we have everything to gain
> and nothing to lose
> by hearing a fresh interpretation
> even of a story we think we know
> inside out.
> Open us to new insights
> knowledge, wisdom
> truth and peace
> wherever you have put these
> in our path.

With love, Daddy

Dear Chris,

How right you are Chris, when you say that the Bible is an amazing book! It surely is! I still have my Gideon Bible, which was given to me at my secondary school in 1967. I used to read it at night and put it under my pillow — I am sure my parents thought I was strange, but they never stopped me reading the Bible. The Qur'an evokes similar feelings for me but the basic difference is that, whereas the Bible has gone through evolution in some ways, the Qur'an remains in the same language as it was revealed. Of course, Arabic is not my language and I have difficulty understanding it. Therefore, to grasp what the Qur'an says I have to go back to the English translation.

I often wonder if your Liberation Theologians are the ones who contextualise the Bible for today? If this is correct, then the follow-up question has to be, can there be another way? Wouldn't any religion have problems if theology was to get stuck in time? Religion has to be contextualised and without this religion is no more than a blind following!

I often wonder why God chose the East to send his messages for humanity, and not the West. Does this mean that the West was in darkness?

Indeed, the Sri Lankan interpretation of the Magi story is revolutionary, and no doubt it is difficult for many to digest in the Western church. I wonder how much of Western dominated interpretations arise as a backdrop from the colonisation of the 'darker' world. Maybe we need to pray and hope for a world that can bring East and West to see the light at the end of the tunnel.

'Hope is being able to see that there is light despite all the darkness.' — Archbishop Emeritus Desmond Tutu

Yours, Anjum

Wednesday 21 December

Dear Jonny,

While mummy pulls things together in the run-up to Christmas – I dread to think what it would be like for you if it was all left to me! – and your excitement builds, there're a few things that I need to pull together before we reach the big day.

Let's come back to Matthew a bit later because we've had a few days of him already this week.

You'll remember that Luke paints a diptych – a two-sided painting – to show religious insiders on the one hand and outsiders on the other, and the way in which they keep relating to one another and being brought together. Well, Luke has a couple more stories to offer of this sort in his second chapter (verses 21 to 52).

Like John the Baptist before him, Jesus is named. But Luke doesn't make such a literal 'song and dance' out of this as he did before, or even as Matthew does with his focus on Jesus being named by Joseph. Luke's focus, instead, is on the moment when Mary and Joseph take Jesus up to the temple to make the sacrifice that they had to do according to religious law. The focus of this was, at one level, the mother. There's a feast on 2 February each year that's called Candlemas when this story is told in full. But it's also called the Purification. It's about Mary being made clean, or blessed, after having given birth.

But as well as this having a practical reason – Mary being cleansed and blessed – and, also, being the chance to give thanks for the birth of a baby, it also gives Luke another chance to strengthen his outsider-insider theme.

We see Mary and Joseph, the young, peasant outsiders from the country who are far from the centres of political and religious influence and power. We see them come to the city of Jerusalem, which is the city at the centre of it all and the most important place for politics and religion. They come to meet two elderly insiders who are like Elizabeth and Zechariah. These new insiders have been waiting for the fulfilment of something. And this something we might quite properly call God's dream. That's what Archbishop Emeritus Desmond Tutu calls it.

Behind all that I've written has been God's dream of a world where everyone knows the oneness of all of us. It's this oneness for which Simeon and Anna have been waiting their whole lives: the longed-for Messiah who will set everyone free to enjoy their oneness in God. All over the world Anjum and I have seen people waiting for this. For example, Grace in Nairobi said that she'd been waiting her whole life to be shown God's call to love her Muslim neighbours. It was so humbling for us when she said that our workshop had been the moment of Epiphany. Or I could tell you of the imam in Zanzibar who had suffered terribly for spending his life encouraging Muslims to learn about their Christian neighbours and to see the image of God in them. He could have given up. But he refused to cease working for the better humanity he knew *Allah* (that's just the Arabic word for God, the same God in whom we believe) wanted for all. Or what about the young woman in Sri Lanka who'd been trafficked (that means she'd been made a slave – yes, a slave in the twenty-first century!)? She was receiving help to put her life right and she was also helping other young women to do the same. Then there is the priest in South Africa, Fr Michael Lapsley, whose hands were blown off when he received a letter bomb. But he's given the rest of his life to helping people come to terms with some of the terrible things that have happened to them. All these people, and so many, many more, have held fast to the hope that God's dream will come true.

Somehow, across the crowded temple forecourt, Simeon and Anna saw Mary and Joseph and knew that their child was the Messiah. They didn't say that everything would be plain sailing for him. As we've seen in these stories, and as every parent the world over will tell you, the joy of new life is always tempered with the anxiety of responsibility and the desire to protect and nurture new life so that a child may fulfil her or his dreams.

You may remember the crest of Blackburn Cathedral. It's a human heart pierced by a sword. This used to fascinate you as a very much smaller child. That symbolism comes from this story and what Simeon said to Mary, which was that a sword would pierce her heart. Things would be tough for Jesus – and also tough for his mother because to watch your child suffer is the agony that no parent ever, ever wants. Suffering is a part of the tough yet rich mystery of life, as so many of the people Anjum and I have met would testify. But it's not the end of the story.

The last people we heard singing in Luke's story were angels. Simeon isn't sprightly like them! He's ancient. But he can muster a song nonetheless. It's one of the two that Anglicans use in their evening prayer. It's a song of fulfilment. It's known by its Latin title, *Nunc dimittis*:

> Lord, now lettest thou they servant depart in peace
> according to thy word.

For mine eyes have seen
thy salvation;
which thou hast prepared
before the face of all people;
to be a light to lighten the Gentiles

and to be the glory of thy people Israel.

I've been singing this since I was about six. That's a very long time, I know. I said that before you did! And I typed the old English words because that's how I learned to sing them every day for so many years of my life. It's a song that's got that central Advent image, light conquering darkness. This is because, as in the words of the fourth Gospel writer, John, this light of Jesus can never be overcome. But it's also got some of the central themes we've been uncovering together. It's about *all* people getting a chance to share in this light, not just some. Jesus is light and love, and Lord and King for Gentiles and Jewish folk alike. He's God's dream made human.

Jesus' parents must have been confused by all the fuss. They take him away and he grows up back on the margins in Nazareth. That's enough taste of the temple and insider life for one day. They bring him back when he's twelve and Jesus the outsider sits with the insiders who can teach him the faith. He sits as each of us must with our elders in the faith and what he says surprises his teachers. Jesus gets so carried away that he forgets that he must leave with his parents and they have to go back to fetch him. Not that you'd do anything like that, go off and do your own thing without telling mummy and me...

But the next time he's back at the centre it won't be to run rings round his teachers as an early show of independence. The next time will be for real. It will be so that God's dream may come true.

God of our dreams,
you set before us a Kingdom
to hope for
and a way of life
to walk in.
The waiting can be so long
and the birth can be difficult.
But we know that the light is there.
Draw us to its brightness
nurture us by its warmth
and kindle in each of us
the transforming fire of your love.

With love, Daddy

Dear Chris,

Christmas is almost here and up goes the Christmas tree! I'm told that the tree has little to do with the Christian story. But I remember making my own Christmas tree when I was little – and what a beautiful tree it was too!

The story of all those people we met in faraway lands reminds me of those who are closer to home. I'm reminded of the likes of David and Liz Gould, who lost their daughter in the 7/7 bombings or Lisa French, who sat behind the bomber on the bus when it was blown up in the London bombings. All three are Christians and they are fighting for a just world. I'm also reminded of the likes of Moazzam Begg, the ex-Guantanamo detainee who was arrested twice and his mind, body and soul were tortured for a crime he did not commit. But he is someone who believes in lighting a candle instead of cursing the darkness. All these people are not rich and famous. Nevertheless, because they have faith in God's plan, they are guided towards the light. These people are just like the Magi who were guided by the star and the shepherds who were told to find the one who is the light.

All these people who come from different parts of the world worship one God in different ways. They believe that God's truth will rescue us all from darkness.

We need to remember that darkness is the absence of light; therefore, we need to search for the light and follow the star!

'In order for the light to shine so brightly, the darkness must be present.' – Francis Bacon

Yours, Anjum

Thursday 22 December

Dear Jonny,

One of the problems with the season of Advent is that we get so distracted by all the preparations for celebrating Christmas. We don't always make enough room to contemplate what this season.

Not all of this is actually bad. The pressure in our part of the world to buy more and more presents and spend more and more money at this time is crippling. When I think of the many places that Anjum and I visited, I feel terrible about the way we in Britain just throw money at Christmas. It's not the wish for happiness that's wrong, of course; but we can't think that spending money can buy us happiness.

When I was studying to be a priest, I read a little book called *Christmas Eve* by a German Christian, Friedrich Schleiermacher. It's a lovely little story in which he contrasts all the men of the household sitting around discussing what the coming of Jesus means while all the women prepare the food for Christmas. It was written about one hundred and fifty years ago. It has – to our ears and eyes – a very sexist way of looking at things, with women doing the cooking and men doing the thinking. But, interestingly, Schleiermacher is very much with the women. They are – he suggests – the ones who have the real experience of Christmas, because they are trying to create the warmth that will mean everyone gets to experience the love which is at the heart of Christmas. It's the experience, the feeling, the love that matters most. As an English poet, Christina Rossetti, who lived at the same time of Schleiermacher puts it: 'Love came down at Christmas, love all lovely, love divine.' That's what we need to focus on. As one of the songs of the pop group the Beatles suggests, money can't buy me love. Nothing indeed, can buy it. We can only make room for it. And, as you know from once being the inn-keeper in a nativity play, making room for Jesus is right at the heart of the story. Every parent expecting a baby has to make room for all that follows a birth: the endless nappy-changing, the feeding and the sleepless nights; but also the amazing cuddles and kisses, the smiles and gurgles, and the delight of looking into sparkling eyes. A newborn changes everything!

It's very hard to make room to hear the story of Christmas amid all the preparations. I remember, as I've mentioned before, bishop John V Taylor explaining how the only way he could focus on Christmas each year was to write a poem that gave him the space, not only to think about what it meant, but what it made him feel. Earlier in these letters I shared one of these poems. Now I'd like to share another. It's called *Diptych* – not the diptych we've been exploring in Luke with its depiction of the two babies, John and Jesus, and their parents. This time the diptych takes the image of space that we find at both ends of the life of Jesus – the space of the womb in Mary within which he grew, and the space of the tomb within which his body was laid after he died. By weaving them together this poem tries to show how Christian belief is all about new life bursting from a womb and, also, from a grave. It's this life and love which Christmas (and, in fact, Easter) is all about:

He who lay curled in Mary's womb,
starting and ending in a cave,
has broken new-born from the tomb.

His star outshone the smothering gloom,
searching for those he came to save.
He who lay curled in Mary's womb

To take upon himself our doom,
and our unkindnesses forgave,
has broken new-born from the tomb.

Again they offered sweet perfume,
myrrh for his helpless limbs they gave,
he who lay curled in Mary's womb.

Swaddling allows too little room;
he that was bound from crib to grave
has broken new-born from the tomb.

Angels again brought tidings: 'Whom
sleekest thou? See, the Lord you crave,
he who lay curled in Mary's womb,
has broken new-born from the grave.'

One year I set this poem to music in the week running up to
Christmas. A choir in Cambridge had asked me for something
and, though it drove mummy mad (what with me banging out
the same melodies and harmonies over and over again!), it helped
me really to think about how to make room for Jesus and what it
felt like to have him at the centre of my life. This year I'll try to
do something less annoying for everyone by making some space
to remember the people Anjum and I met on our travels. I shall
think about what Christmas might feel like for them – perhaps,
now that you've heard some of their stories, you can join me?

Loving God,
as the Christmas scene
gets filled with the junk
by which we fill
every available space:
help us to slow down
to pause
to stop
to look
to listen
to the sight and sound
of divine love.
You always have space for us
in your heart
help us to unclutter our lives
and make space for you.

With love, Daddy

Dear Chris,

Ah! The market values taking over our lives! Yes, sadly, Christmas is not what it used to be. I can remember when we were very little and used to have proper white winters. My neighbours would take me along with them when they went carol singing. It seems like another time — when children sat around listening to the stories about the Nativity and I used to love watching Robert Powell in Jesus of Nazareth... Where has all that gone? Today, Christmas trees go up too early and our malls and arcades bustle with shoppers laden with bags of shopping.

Chris, do you remember us visiting Nairobi? In the slums of Kibera walking was unbearable because of stench from the gutters, yet one million people live and survive on $1 a day. Have we Muslims and Christians lost the ability to remember our religious festivals as celebrations with families, friends and neighbours? Instead, we rush off to the sales and queue overnight for the right bargains! I see changes in my own faith communities too, where once mums would get up early in the morning and head straight for the kitchen, and the men would go to the mosques for Eid prayers. The female members of the family would be dressed in colourful clothing, preparing delicious food and we kids could not wait for the men folk to come back from the mosques, so that we could get our presents (mostly given in cash, as was the tradition). Today, on Eid days, our young people hire big cars and drive down the streets with music blaring without any concern for the communities. The heart of the story of Eid seems to have been forgotten — it was never meant to be celebrated in big cars on the streets, just as Christmas was never meant to be about presents alone!

> 'Then the Grinch thought of something he hadn't before! What if Christmas, he thought, doesn't come from a store? What if Christmas...perhaps...means a little bit more!' — Dr Seuss, How the Grinch Stole Christmas!

Yours, Anjum

Friday 23 December

Dear Jonny,

A few years before making these journeys you've been reading about, Anjum and I went to the Holy Land with the BBC. There were six of us: two Christians, two Jews and two Muslims. We were there to make a week's worth of radio programmes which would take people to religious sites important to the three faiths. We were not only hoping to allow people to see why these sites mattered but, also, to give them a glimpse of how one person's holy space might well have come about at the expense of another's. So, for instance, the space in front of the Western Wall – so sacred to the Jewish people – was made possible by the bulldozing of Christian and Muslim Palestinian houses.

The idea was to interview representatives of the faiths. We were hoping to get to the heart of what causes conflict between them and what might bring about peace.

On one afternoon we spoke with a Jewish settler who was an Israeli citizen. This is a person who has built a home on disputed land. The United Nations says that it belongs to the Palestinians, the state of Israel says that it belongs to them. She was a lovely woman, kind and hospitable, gracious in the time that she spent with us. But, by the end of it, we all – including her Jewish compatriots – agreed that she could not understand another person's point of view.

We moved on to interview a Muslim man who is a professor at Al-quds University. We met him over a meal. He was very charming and, again, gracious with his time. But behind the smiles we all detected a steeliness which meant that when we pushed him during the questions we again sensed that he could not put himself in someone else's shoes.

By now we were a little down-hearted. We moved to the Anglican cathedral in Jerusalem, St George's Cathedral, just outside the Old City. Here we met an Anglican priest, Hosam Naoum, who was, then, the priest to the Palestinian congregation; now, he is the dean of the cathedral. We had, to be honest, almost given up on the interviewing. But as our technical team produced the microphones, something so unexpected happened it simply bowled us over.

Fr Hosam was born in a village which, though Palestinian at the time of the birth of the state of Israel in 1948, was eventually declared Israeli. This meant that all the villagers received Israeli passports. The woman he married, however, came from a village which was categorised differently. She had Palestinian papers. So when, later, Fr Hosam was appointed to the staff of the cathedral, he could come to work their straight away – but his wife and their two children had to remain for two years in a village outside Jerusalem whilst the authorities, cruelly, delayed the day when they could all live together.

Fr Hosam told the story with passion, but without a trace of bitterness. Indeed, he freely acknowledged that he understood Israeli concerns about security. He had so emptied himself of his own feelings and opinions that he was able totally to make space for someone else's perspective. There are only two other people whom I've met who've been able to do this so convincingly: they are the South Africans Nelson Mandela and Desmond Tutu.

One of the people in the party – I cannot remember whether Jew or Muslim – made the startling remark, 'We don't have this quality in our religion.' No one said a word for we all knew that we had reached a moment of amazing vulnerability and truth, the sort of moment that perhaps only comes once or twice in a lifetime. Silence fell. God had spoken.

At Christmas this self-emptying God, who speaks in many ways, comes to us in Jesus Christ.

When the earliest Christians wanted to express the astonishing truth of the self-emptying God they put it in a hymn. We find it in St Paul's letter to some of the earliest Christians in a place called Philippi (chapter 2:5-11). Many people think it's the oldest Christian hymn or creed (that means statement of belief) there is. Morna Hooker, a professor who taught me, used to describe it as a V shape. At the top of the left side of the V is God in heaven who empties himself and takes the form of a servant coming to earth – the middle of the V. This is so that, accepting death for us on the cross and giving us a share in his Resurrection, through baptism into his body, he could lift us to join him at the top of the right hand of the V in heaven:

> Let the same mind be in you that was in Christ Jesus,
> who, though he was in the form of God,
> did not regard equality with God
> as something to be exploited,
> but emptied himself,
> taking the form of a slave,
> being born in human likeness.
> And being found in human form,

he humbled himself
and became obedient to the point of death —
even death on a cross.

Therefore God also highly exalted him
and gave him the name
that is above every name,
so that at the name of Jesus
every knee should bend,
in heaven and on earth and under the earth,
and every tongue should confess
that Jesus Christ is Lord,
to the glory of God the Father.

It takes us back to the idea of creating space, which we talked about yesterday, and the need to empty ourselves to make room for God and for our neighbours. It invites us to stand in someone else's shoes and to see things through their eyes, which is perhaps the most important lesson we re-learned on our travels. And this is the lesson which God wishes to teach us all, of whatever faith or world view, in Jesus Christ.

Open God,
make us attentive
to the experience
of those whom we meet.
Give us the grace
to let them speak
in their own words
to tell their own story
before butting-in with our own.
Help us to see things
from their perspective

as you saw things from ours
in order to bring us home.
With love, Daddy

Dear Chris,

I remember the '3 Faiths Pilgrimage' to Jerusalem as if it was yesterday. I recall the Jewish settler and the Muslim professor and, of course, Fr Hosam, to whom I presented a reproduction of the Blackburn Pax (which shows a depiction of Mary that worshippers kissed when they shared the sign of peace). There was another incident which has stayed with me too. It was the Jewish lecturer from the Hebrew University of Jerusalem. When I extended my hand in friendship to her, she pulled her hand back. This was witnessed by all, the BBC crew and members of our group! I could have walked away and put it down to 'bad experience'. But as someone who has always believed in getting down to the difficult conversations I said to her that her action will not change me towards her — should she be in trouble I will be the first one to help her, as dictated by my faith. At this point she put her arms over my shoulders and said, 'I think I can work with you.' Jewish people have been persecuted and the Palestinians are today paying the price of the Holocaust. Their oppression cannot be denied! How can one build a Holocaust memorial like Yad Vasham on a piece of land that saw demolition of homes of Palestinians?

I recall sitting in the gardens of St. George's Cathedral when Fr Hosam told us about the injustice perpetuated by the Israelis and how his wife could not join him for two years because of paperwork. Where is the justice in keeping families apart? Yes, it was Fr Hosam's story; but the way he told it, without any hatred for those who have done him wrong, made tears swell up in my eyes and I got a lump in my throat!

How can we have peace if we do not listen to each other? How can we have peace if we do not create space to have difficult conversations? Without conversations there can never be any peace between faiths.

> 'O you who have believed, be persistently standing firm for Allah, witnesses in justice, and do not let the hatred of a people prevent you from being just. Be just; that is nearer to righteousness. And fear Allah; indeed, Allah is acquainted with what you do.' — Qur'an 5:8

Yours, Anjum

Saturday 24 December

Dear Jonny,

Wow! It's Christmas Eve. Usually things are so frantic for me. But now that I'm not serving as a parish priest but trying to help people training to be one, my Christmas diary is strangely empty and I'm with you and mummy, and your brothers. Don't worry, she won't ask me to do the cooking! That part of Christmas is still safe. Anyway, 'dad's cooking so what do we want from the takeaway?' won't work at this time of year. The takeaway is shut!

I don't know what you'll take away from these letters. I'll look forward to hearing one day when you're older and have a chance to read them. But one of the things I'll take away from writing them is what a privilege it is to have had a chance to share something of the stories and hopes, and challenges and opportunities that Anjum and I have experienced. I hope, like me, that you'll think of all the places and people I've described. Let us pray for them, as I'm sure they'll think and pray for us. That's one of the beauties of oneness that exists already in the global church of which our own Church of England is just one among many expressions. I am also deeply moved to think that people of other faiths are praying for us too, just as we ought to pray for them at their sacred times. One year I saw the imam of Claremont, Rashied Omar, singing 'Hark, the herald angels sing, glory to the newborn king' during the Cape Town Cathedral carol procession – at once I knew that God's dream was just a little closer!

Matthew's gospel story is a bit different to Luke's. It has a different focus as they say. It's for a different audience. Luke focuses on the sword, that will one day pierce Mary's heart. But Matthew (chapter 2 verses 7 to 23) fleshes out some of the immediate dangers.

In Matthew's story, you'll remember that things happen in dreams. We left a very cross Herod a few letters ago. He was about to kill all the boy babies under two year's old because he was so threatened by the Magi and their talk of a newborn king. Chillingly, that all comes to fruition. It's no dream – it's a reality. It sees Mary, Joseph and Jesus being forced to seek asylum in Egypt. Joseph is told in a dream that they must wait there until Herod is dead and it's safe to return. Of course there's symbolism here too: the people of God were led to freedom from slavery in Egypt and it's appropriate that the new Exodus, the new journey to freedom, should also begin from Egypt. Sure enough, later, Joseph is told in another dream to go back, though there's some hesitation in his response because Herod's son, Archelaus, is now reigning. Yet another dream tells Joseph that Galilee is a better bet.

But I don't buy into the symbolic side of this too much. If the journeys that Anjum and I have undertaken have shown us anything, it's that God's dream is too often deferred by people who come up with fancy symbolic and spiritual explanations for stuff that is frankly just too intolerable for words. The symbols can be a way of avoiding harsh realities that need to be tackled not ignored. Yet, however he gets there and whatever weight we place on the symbolism of fleeing to Egypt as asylum seekers, Matthew, like Luke, lands Jesus in Nazareth. From there quite an extraordinary story will unfold!

Gosh, it's almost time for the carol service. I won't write more today because we must now go and hear about an angel arriving in Nazareth to speak to a young girl just a few years older than you ... Well, you know from these letters what that started!

Holy God,
you call us back
to the old story
because, inexhaustibly
in it we discover new truths
about what it means
to be human:
give us sight and insight
this Christmas
to hear your word
to ponder it in our hearts
and to embrace your dream
for us and for all creation.

With love, Daddy

Dear Chris,

A day before the good news! As a family we also celebrated the good news of another birth. My parents had four girls and, as any family, having a son was a big deal. In those days one did not have the facility or the inclination to know what sex one's forthcoming sibling was going to be. My parents had their first baby boy on 24th December, a day before Christmas. He was two months premature, but we were delighted with the new arrival of our baby brother. We had travelled from Pakistan to UK three months before and the journey was long. But the good news for us as a family overcame all that we had to endure in coming to the UK. Every year we four sisters would make sure that our house was decorated with birthday cards and decorations. Lights seem to be the main ingredient for celebrations. We used to decorate our house with beautiful multiple coloured lights, although I must say many of our neighbours thought that we were preparing for Christmas!

Both outsiders, like me, and insiders, like you, bring the forthcoming birth of Jesus, son of Mary / Mariam, alive in our own way. But we both agree that we cannot live without Jesus.

'Christmas is built upon a beautiful and intentional paradox; that the birth of the homeless should be celebrated in every home.' – G.K. Chesterton

Yours, Anjum

Sunday 25 December

Dear Jonny,

It's a boy.

That's what the midwife said when you were born ten minutes after mummy arrived at Blackburn Royal Infirmary. The midwife was a rather strange woman. I thought she was Mrs Doubtfire from the film. She looked the same and her Scottish accent was exactly like Robbie Williams'. She'd actually sent us home a few hours before because she thought that mummy wasn't far enough on in labour. Well, a few hours later, we knew that mummy was almost there and we sent for an ambulance – which took the longest and bumpiest route to the hospital! When we arrived we remembered that the drop-off still meant a very long corridor walk to the delivery suite. To be honest, I had visions of mummy giving birth in that corridor or in the lift. But we made it. And then you emerged! I've never seen mummy more happy than when she held you – except when she held your brothers Dominic and Gregory in the same way of course! And if I fold my arms now as I did when mummy put you in them, or think of the sheer joy on your two brothers' faces as they held you, I find that tears well up and are soon rolling down my face. I do cry a lot, don't I?!

There's nothing in the world like new life. I saw one of the ordinands holding another ordinand's baby the other day and he looked so absolutely still and content, so absorbed and at peace. It was the most beautiful of sights. That's the impact that the mystery we call life has on us at our very best: that is, when we get beyond thinking about ourselves and are just open to the God who comes to us as total gift.

I know that perhaps much of the story Anjum and I discovered has been about us human beings when we are less good – in fact, sometimes, when we are at our worst. Perhaps you're wondering, as many of us do, where things go wrong?

Christmas Day isn't the day for a long discussion of this. The answer, anyway, is a simple one. They go wrong because we lose that sense of openness: that is, the sense that when we hold new life, when we meet a new person, or culture, or faith, or country or continent, we are to receive all this as total gift.

Perhaps, if we try that, each and every day will indeed be filled with the happiness we wish on each other.

That's certainly what I wish for you with all my heart.

Lord Jesus
child of Bethlehem
Son of God the Father,
hold us in the embrace
of your love
as we look into your eyes
and see the reflection of
who each of us truly is:
born to be free,
born for greatness,

born to show your glory
in all the world.
Emmanuel
Saviour of all
be born in us this day
and remain with us for ever
uniting us with one another
in the power of your Holy Spirit.
Happy Christmas!

All my love, Daddy

Dear Chris,

He is here!

As I said in my last response, we were delighted to have a new addition in our family: my youngest brother arrived on Christmas Eve. On Christmas Day everyone is at my parent's home, not because it's Christmas but because it's my father's birthday on 25th December. It is also the birthday of another man who is my role model: Mr Mohammad Ali Jinnah, founding father of Pakistan. For our family, the gathering on the 25th is important as we try to get all the siblings with their children and grandchildren over for dinner. An amazing sight, but not something that I could repeat too frequently! In fact, we have four generations under one roof, and nine years ago we had five – I lost my grandmother who lived to be 100+, bless her. Five Children, 11 grandchildren and 3 great-grandchildren... The noise from humanity is deafening! Subhan Allah (praise to God)!

As I look at my parents and our family, I am compelled to reflect on the fact that we are one humanity. We are one family who have differences of opinions — yet ultimately we are one! Peace to you all!

'The birth of a new born baby creates motherhood, before that we are no more than the other' — Anjum Anwar

Yours, Anjum